MAJESTIC PLEASURES

BY

ADRINA SMITH

Edited and Published by
Creolistic Ink Publishing
Destrehan, LA

ISBN-13: 978-0692873137 (Custom Universal)
ISBN-10: 0692873139

Dedication

To anyone who doesn't know how to let go of someone that has caused heartache. Stop allowing him/her to live rent free in your mind; give them buttery popcorn to enjoy your growth.

Reviews

Majestic Pleasure is one of the MEATIEST books you will EVER read!!!! You will not put it down until the end; it is full of surprises, twists, turns, love and more. Your anticipation will continue to rise to new heights while wanting more. This book is a definite must have and read….

Myia Baker

After reading Pleasurable Acts which I really enjoyed, I could not wait for Majestic Pleasures. This sequel is jaw dropping every time you turned the page. Alexis is the business owner of Thrill Pleasers where all your erotica fantasies becomes a reality and the next moment taking out anyone that crossed her or someone she cared for, with the help of Shafiq her lover. Majestic Pleasure is a page turner from beginning to end and it leaves you in suspense. Adrina is a great writer and I am looking forward to reading her creativity in the future…

Tracey Rogers

Prologue

Months passed and the Congo Square-Louis Armstrong Park prepares for a weekend of jazz and food as we patrol the area.

"Look Man, this bitch has been breathing too long and something needs to be done," says Anthony.

"Shit, I have been trying to see her but she doesn't want anything to do with me," responds Stephen.

"Nigga, you are knee deep in this shit and ain't going nowhere until she is dead. Do you understand me?"

"Yeah, I understand. Have you gotten a call or text from Clarissa?"

"Fuck that weak bitch. I don't have time for her whining ass. She knew about the plan years ago, wanted to fall in love and get sloppy."

"She and I was a mistake. It is not a day that goes by I don't regret getting into this bullshit."

"Did you think about regret when you were fucking the bottom out? Save the righteousness for church."

"Wait a damn minute, it is not my fault Bianca sold her ass in college."

"Stick to the motherfucking plan or be in a body bag."

"You don't get it. I am still in love with Alexis."

"Shut the hell up! I don't give a fuck about how you feel. Get rid of her or I will get rid of you," says Anthony while pointing the 9mm to his head.

“Calm down, we are supposed to be boys. Put the fucking gun down before somebody gets hurt. I will do it; I need more time.”

“You have two months. She is walking around rebuilding her life with no regards of how mine was destroyed.”

“The problem is Bianca not Alexis, can’t you see it?”

“No nigga, they took my happiness. I will deal with Alexis then Bianca. Both of them hoes ain’t shit and will regret fucking over me.”

“I hear you but holding a grudge all of these years is a lot to carry. You need to speak to a psychiatrist or someone; this shit is getting out of hand.”

“Man, fuck you and your hand. Are we still on for pool tonight?’

“How the hell you are gonna threaten me then wanna shoot pool. Your ass is crazy, let me call home and make sure.”

“I don’t understand how the hell you cry about being in love with Alexis, fucking Clarissa and married this chick after a few months.”

How long before the skeletons are clothed and exposed.

Chapter 1

(Alexis)

One year has passed and Majestic Pleasures is the place for unadulterated debauchery. Beautiful bookstore located in the *Vieux Carre`* district serving beignets, coffee and wine with smooth sounds of jazz.

Watching the patrons during the day transform to characters at night always stimulate my appetite.

I need a break from scanning 100 applications. It can be very tiresome however the stature of ThrillPleasers and my image are at stake.

Sitting in my office listening to *Tamia "Stuck with Me,"* with eyes close and legs open. I place my left foot on the cherry wood desk, right hand finds my stem and holding tight to the back of the chair. I slowly rotate my hips as the thought of Shafiq motherfucking chin is covered with my pear juice…Oh My Goodness…Yes…YE….

"Hey Alex, Bianca said it was okay to come in," a male voice interrupts.

"What the fuck?" I yell.

"Surprise?"

"Damn right I am surprised! Have a seat in the lobby and I will be with you in a minute."

Scramble through the bottom drawer for my shea butter baby wipes and call Bianca with anger, "Ms McWright, come here!" I hear rattled paper then clacked running heels.

She knocks, peeks in and asks, "Boss Lady, did I do something wrong?"

"Bianca, don't send no damn body to my office without giving notice. I was trying to get a fucking nut when he barged in."

"We talked two hours before I sent him. I noticed you didn't go to lunch; thought it would be a nice surprise."

"Yeah another secret."

We laugh as I flatten my skirt and straighten my blouse. She leaves to get him from the lobby as I sit at my desk.

"Wow Alex, that is a wonderful way to say you miss me."

"Hello Keith," I respond with a big hug.

"I swear you are still good on the eyes."

"I am sure you didn't come to look at me. What's going on?"

"I am the new Director of Operations at the Avondale Shipyard."

"Okay? Why are you here? You could have left a message or sent an email."

"Alex, you are the only woman who truly knows me. Let's have dinner to catch up on old times."

"I thought that is what we are doing? We can do lunch next week, get with Bianca to arrange it. Sorry to cut this short but I have a meeting. It was nice to see you again."

We stand, he kisses my cheek and leaves.

Damn, that fucking man still soaks my panties. I better stay away from him.

Gather my briefcase and smell the aftermath of his cologne on my clothes. I imagine my mouth speaking French to his hard and melted chocolate stick.

Backtracking to my desk to retrieve my purse, "I have to take control of this monkey on my shoulder."

Clutch my phone and call Shafiq, "Hey Behbee, I am leaving the office but extremely hungry."

"Hey My Love, do your thang and Eye will see u later. Hungry huh? I'll think of something to feed u."

"I love when you talk like that. See you later, love you."

"Love u moor."

Walk to the front door and announce, "Hey Bianca, I will be in *Plaquemines Parish* for the afternoon."

"I confirmed your meeting with the secretary five minutes ago, and the client is looking forward to it."

"Wow, more flowers from your secret admirer?" I smile seeing them on the counter.

"I am not interested. A real man would deliver them himself," she answers with disgust and throws six long stemmed red roses in the trash.

"Maybe he or she is shy," laughing at her facial expression.

"You can't be shy with me. I prefer aggression." She says smacking her ass.

"Who's in charge tonight?"

"Veronica because I have two appointments."

"Please remind her to set the alarm at 5:30 am," candidly mentions and close the door.

I drive in silence for two hours and arrive at a 100-year-old home turned upscale restaurant named Le Bon Temps House. A staff member greets me at the door with a glass of champagne.

"You must be Ms. Roulle, Mrs. Fountaine is waiting on you," he states escorting me to the table.

A fucking light skinned, green eyes, naturally curly hair with wide hips woman, ummmmmm."

"Hel-lo Ms. Roulle, my name is Camille. It is a pleasure to finally meet you." She introduces in a thick Creole accent.

"Hi, I thought I was having lunch with a man." I reply with embarrassment.

"My secretary is famous for leaving out pertinent information. I will speak to Stacy about it when I get back to my office but I hope it doesn't change doing business?"

"Not at all."

"Good. Forgive the emptiness of the restaurant; I paid for complete privacy. I am very discreet of all of my endeavors and didn't want to share your time with the rest of the world."

"I truly understand." I answer with a brow slightly raised.

"Have a seat, the menu has been ordered. We will start with alligator balls, scallops and oysters; salad with blackened chicken, strawberries and blue cheese dressing, shrimp and beef tenderloin topped off with dessert."

"That sounds wonderful."

Chef Gerard comes with a table side presentation of his special coffee; Crème de Cocoa, Grand Marnier, rum and chocolate syrup garnished by a flaming orange peel.

"Mrs. Fountaine, thank you for seeing me on short notice. Are you aware of what my company provides?"

"Ms. Roulle, I have been following your career for quite a while and you have a very prestigious operation. I can definitely become one of your valuable clients."

"May I ask what have you covered?"

"Be assured Alexis, nothing is done overnight and I know your past. I am impressed with your status and the path you walk to keep it shall I say cultivated."

I smile opening the briefcase and laying the documents on the table, "Nothing happens until the application is approved, favorable background and credit check."

"I will have all of the paperwork by the end of the week, I am looking for excitement," she admits flipping through the documents.

She is beyond ready for my expertise but eager; that is a good and bad thing.

The huge plate of bananas, crème puffs, chocolate sauce and other layers of goodness paired to *Leflaive's Puligny-Montrachets* perfect sweet white wine excites my palate.

"I am looking for a thriving agency to fulfill all of my strangest inhibitions and I know you can feed the urge. I am interested in starting our relationship today." She mentions licking the sauce from her fingers.

"Slow down, Mrs. Fountaine. The process takes up to three months but call me early next week to setup a tour."

"Three months? Can you expedite my process?"

"Are you aware the basic thrill starts at $5,000?"

She stands, walks over to my seat and slides her hands in my blouse.

"I am aware of many things," she whispers in my ear while pinching my nipples.

I grab her wrists and state, "I have the perfect person for you but it will cost $7,500."

She walks to her chair, obtain an envelope from her purse and responds, "I am ready for my first session; the rest is a bonus."

Open the envelope and count 100 *Benjamin Franklins*, "Guess we are in business. Next weekend is the earliest but it will be worth the wait."

Wonderful way to start and end the day.... Satisfied..

Chapter 2

The ride home is stop and go from the accident on *I-10*. Some people can't seem to keep their eyes on the road.

Finally make it to my condo and I am mentally exhausted. The only thing I want to do is… relax.

Put the keys in the door and hear music with a hint of food. Stand in the entrance of the living room and admire Shafiq dancing with a towel wrapped around his waist.

Tiptoe in the kitchen to surprise him but he quickly turns around and says, "You really need to work on your ninja skills," as he kisses my forehead.

"Okay, funny guy. What are you cooking?" I ask peeking over his shoulder.

"Didn't u mention being hungry earlier. Eye cooked Curry Chicken and Dumplings, white rice, cabbage and your favorite *Ruby Relaxer* as a celebration.

"Damn, I was referring to dick Behbee. I guess my stomach can handle a little taste. Did you say celebration?"

"Yes, My Love. Freshen up and join me in 20 minutes."

Twitch my tail to the bedroom and look for something to wear. Undress, wash, soak in a bubble filled jetted tub and soak the end to another workday.

Unsure of the time passed when Shafiq hollers, "Alex, u forget about me. Come on!"

I jump from the water and say, "I must have drifted off. I am sorry."

"Hurry up, Eye don't want to miss it."

I quickly put on a *Purple Harlow Satin Kimono Robe* and *Karlie Crotchless Laced Thong with a Bow* from *Fredericks of Hollywood.*

I walk in the living room and the coffee table has plates, candles and poured wine.

He turns on the TV and says, "Sit down and eat. Eye want to show u something."

"Are we watching porn?"

"No, My Love but it will get u wet. I promise."

"YYYYYAAAAAAYYYYYY!!!"

Ms. Toussaint rearranges her hair and reports on WHFY Channel 3 News, "The tragic accident on *I-10* by *Veterans Blvd* exit has confirmed one death. The red GMC Yukon drove into a guardrail after hitting other cars before exploding. The deceased person has been confirmed as 47-year-old Officer Michael Young. He was a veteran of the *Orleans Parish Prison.* The other victims have been transported to *East Jefferson General Hospital* with non-threatening injuries."

I stop eating and say, "Shafiq, I saw a fire truck and three *Jefferson Parish Police* cars on my way home."

"Do u like your gift?" He asks rubbing my cheeks.

"Gift? What the hell are you talking about?"

"Eye will get rid of everyone who hurts u Alexis, everyone!"

I take a long gulp of white wine and reply, "Behbee, in time all of the nonsense will be a distant memory."

I sling the pillows on the floor, look under the sofa and asks, "I don't see anything. Where did you hide it?"

He throws me on the sofa and yells, "Woman! Eye got rid of Michael for u."

I calmly respond, “Oh shit, thank you. Wait a minute, the news said…”

“Accidents are the perfect murder My Love.”

He pulls me closer, tilts my head and slowly unties my robe. Kiss my neck to my left hip then removes my thongs with his teeth.

“Eye love u so much Alex,” whispering to my velvet tip as he undresses.

His tongue begins to play with my hood and clit adagio. Licking up and down until my juices flow in seconds. He covers my mound and blows repeatedly. Spreading my legs wider as he admires the glistening of my lips. He introduces my love tunnel to three fingers and continuously flutter kicks his tongue across my stem.

“Ummmmm,ummmmmm,” I moan seductively.

I pull his face to mine and suck his lips tasting the sweetness of my pear.

He returns to his sexual adventure by tantalizing my pussy and entering my valley. I wrap one leg around his back and the other on his shoulder as he thrusts my insides.

“Everything Eye do is for u,” he mentions through deep breaths and strokes.

He arches my back and intensely touch the heart of my femininity. Gracefully sucking my toes without missing a limb. He passionately gyrates into a finger eight until my body tingles from his existence.

I slap his face and he smiles with a “what the fuck” look.

“Tonight, the sensual shit is for the birds. I want you to slaughter this pussy.”

He grips my dreads then my feet touch my earlobes.

"Yes, that's how I want to be fucked."

He covers my mouth and shoves his inches in my guts.

"Do u love me?" He asks pounding to the bottom of my center.

"Y.E.S," I respond gasping as his scrotum knocks against my labia.

"Cum!" he demands.

I sense a trickle of a squirt when a buzz interrupts my euphoria. He hits my g-spot harder and harder as the noise increases my attention.

He stops and mumbles, "Who the hell is that?"

"Fuck em, don't stop. Shit, don't stop."

Minutes later an erratic knock on the front door spoils our orgasm.

He runs to the bedroom and I hurriedly snatch my robe.

I look through the peep hole and open the door, "Why the fuck is you at my house without calling. This shit betta be important."

"Alexis, I am so sorry but I came over as soon as I got the information."

"Veronica, are you finished with your client?"

"Yes, I am but this couldn't wait until tomorrow."

"What is it?" I ask with crossed arms.

"I got a call from one of the detectives. They found Clarissa's purse with her cell phone and car keys in *City Park* three days ago." She answers with excitement.

"Give me a few minutes to straighten up."

"By the look of things, I interrupted something."

"It's okay. Have a seat."

I walk in the bedroom and Shafiq lies in the bed with a hard dick thumping to my heartbeat.

"Behbee, I am so sorry. Join me in the shower for a quickie so I can find out what's going on."

"Eye got one better." He says pulling me into the bathroom.

He eats the coating off my pussy as the hot water runs and I whimper through his tongue laps. He washes my neck, breasts and downwards without losing sight of my prize.

He tastes from behind as the soap flows down my back.

I tightly hold the rod and within minutes we climax.

He bites my left shoulder and instructs while smacking my ass, "Get dress and I'll straighten up."

I quickly beautify in a *Navy High-Rise Wide Leg Cropped Trouse*r with a *White Over-Sized Gauge Front Shirt* and *Navy Open-Toe Mules* from *Old Navy.*

I meet Veronica in the living room and she is on the floor crying.

"Please stop crying, everything will be okay. I tell you what? Let's get a quick drink and talk at *Daiquiri's & Company*."

"Thank you so much. It has been too long without a word from her and I know something is wrong."

I respond while locking the door. "She has gone on excursions before but we will get through it together."

I really despise emotional bitches

Chapter 3
(Shafiq)

I hate coming to the house and Alexis' scent isn't in the air. She makes everything worthwhile.

Sit on the sofa, turn on the monitors and relax. It was a perfect idea to move Clarissa since Alexis found out about the affair.

I focus on the master bedroom monitor and watch Clarissa standing in the middle of the floor, crying and pulling her hair. I wonder if she is at her breaking point. Alexis invested in this beautiful home and turned it into a business; it is unfortunately blood will be shed.

I wait for darkness to take over for my visit. I cross the street without being seen. Slowly enter the house from the backdoor; creep into the kitchen, then the bedroom.

She sleeps comfortably in the bed as a smile crosses her mouth and it pisses me off instantly.

I dump piss from the bucket on the side and say, "Bitch what the fuck u grinning for? I should kill u right now."

She jumps and screams, "What the hell is going on? Why are you doing this? Whatever Alexis told you isn't true. I can give you double to what she is paying you. Please let me go!!"

I slap her and laugh, "If this was about Alexis, u would have been dead months ago, since u are ungrateful about life, I guess starvation should be your cause of death."

"I am not ungrateful. I love Alexis like a sister. I don't know why she hates me?"

"Bitch, you are delusional! Maybe a growling stomach an idea of betrayal."

"My stomach has never growled with my services," she admits opening her legs.

"Girl, you have got to be out of your motherfucka mind with your funky ass pussy. You can't offer me kibbles in bits when I eat filet mignon. Besides when Stephen left Alexis for you, he showed me a rainbow."

"I can make you feel better than a rainbow. I can bring you the heavens."

"Bitch the only thing to be brought is a present in a fucking hatbox. Off with your head!" I respond with a cutting motion. "I might let you take a shower before killing you; think about those services."

"This shit is about Stephen? He said she was okay with our relationship. Oh my goodness, what the fuck have I done?"

"Look, I don't care about that bullshit. You fucked over her and will beg for every breath."

"If I put my sweetness around your manhood it can change your mind. Please."

I walk closer, unzip my pants and ram my dick in her mouth, "Don't touch me! Suck until I tell you to stop!"

Plop my foot on the footboard and make her gag out the alphabet.

She moans and plays in her pussy.

I yank my dick out, snatch her face and say, "Hoe, this ain't about you. Move your fucking hand."

"It feels so good, let me get mine."

Force it back in and blurt out, "If you touch yourself, I will kill you."

As she sucks deeper and deeper, I think of Alexis caressing my balls. The mere thought of her fills my shaft. I slice her neck from ear to throat as small amount of cum releases; pull out my dick and tightly squeeze the jugular vein to catch the blood.

"Breathe slowly but if you panic it's your fault." I whisper watching her fluid slide between my fingers. My dick goes from hard to soft to steel at the sight of the excitement.

I place her hand over her neck and say, "Be right back."

The fear in her eyes cause my veins to pulsate. Pull up my pants, run to my house, dump the junk drawer for the first aid kit and head back. I notice she is going into shock.

Pour half a liter of *Heaven Hill Bourbon* down her mouth and the rest on her wound as I stitch her up and divulge, "A little gash to remind u who is in charge."

Leave out the backdoor and quickly take a shower at home. My heart trembles while snatching the vibrating phone from the dresser.

"Hey Behbee," she speaks softly.

"Hey My Love. I miss u."

"Behbee, you haven't been gone a whole day but I miss you too," she admits laughing.

"See u in a few." I return the laugh and hang up.

I sneak in to see her fast asleep naked as if she didn't speak to me earlier.

I snatch the covers, get on my knees and eat her pussy while her arms are clasped in mine. She knows it is no escaping. She assumes the position, sucks her dick and enjoys our reversible 69 without question.

She wraps her legs around my neck and does a hand stand without missing a slurp.

Fuck, I love this woman!!!!

Push her down on all fours, grab a handful of dreads with my right hand and set the head of my dick at the tip of her opening.

"Behbee, give it to me."

"Give you what?"

"My dick."

"This dick," as I pull harder; rubbing up and down her clit.

"Shhhhh, stop playing."

She moves the pillows out of the way, open her legs wider and spread her cheeks.

"Fuck me or go to sleep."

That is my cue.

I bust her pussy with an attitude. Whether soaked or dry, it didn't matter to me. In my mind, it was the scene played earlier with Clarissa. Fucking cunt think she can seduce me.

"Next time bitch, it will be deeper. U hear me bitch."

"What a fucking minute. Who are you talking too?"

"Shut the fuck up!"

Place my left hand around her neck and chokes, "Bitch, shut your fucking mouth!"

Stroking deeper and deeper but moans turn into screams.

She flops on the bed a few minutes later, turns over, slaps me and yells, "What the fuck is wrong with you?"

"Oh my goodness Alexis, I am so sorry. I thought you were Clarissa?"

"What the fuck you mean? You fucked that hoe?"

"Hell no! She wanted me but I slashed her throat. Baby, I thought of u when she tried it and got rock hard. Don't be mad at me, please."

She hugs and passionately kisses me, "Behbee, I am not mad."

Tears falls from my eyes because of the disappointment and lay my head on her shoulder in shame.

She moves her hand from my crown and caresses my dick until it stiffens more than wood. Wraps her legs around my back and inserts it in her hole.

"Make your pussy talk behbee."

The Gulf of Mexico would be in disbelief of her wetness.

Our motions match the sound of the music to the mattress.

"Eye love u Alexis."

"Love me more and kill her."

Cumming and premeditating murder is priceless.

Chapter 4

(Alexis)

It is very unusual to be at work before Bianca but I am sure there is a reason for her tardiness.

Walk to the mini *Café de Monde* inside the bookstore, clear my throat and sings, "*I think I betta call Tyrone. Call em...*"

"Good morning Ms. Roulle. I never get tired of hearing that. Are you having the usual?"

"This is yours if you bring the usual," sliding a $50 bill on the counter and going back to my office.

He serves me an extra-large *Chai Tea Latte* with five individual *Land-o Lakes Half and Half*, a shot of *Grand Marnier* and a Raspberry Filled Beignet cut in squares.

Looking at the tray, "Wow, I am impressed."

"Don't be Ms. Roulle. When I try to do something good, it never last cuz I mess it up in the end."

"Lift your head up. You have been working here for almost eight months. You aren't out there running the corners so if you mess up then clean it and keep it moving."

"I got to go Ms Roulle but thank you." He insists.

"Aww Tyrone, you are more than welcome but believe me; you and I will talk again. Have a good day."

Two hours later, Bianca strolls in yelling on the phone, "What the fuck is wrong with you? Stop calling me." Hangs up and runs to the bathroom.

Time for another rescue mission, fuck. Stroll to the bathroom and she is balling her eyes out.

"Bianca, what is wrong? Talk to me."

"Boss Lady, I have gotten strange calls for two weeks. Once I say hello, a guy moans like he is jacking off."

"What the fuck? Are you serious?"

"Yes, and it is driving me crazy. It happens all hours of the day and night."

"Don't get upset but I need to know. Have you had any private sessions?"

"Fuck no. I have dedicated clients."

Within ten minutes her phone rings from a private number, we stare and she runs into the stall crying.

I answer, "Hello."

Voice replies, "Put Bianca on the phone hoe."

Laughing through my words, "If you want her so bad, come get her bitch."

"When I do it's for both of you cum swallowing hoes."

"Don't forget to swipe your mama's throat first motherfucka," I hang up and stomp on the phone.

"Oh Shit! Bianca, I owe you a new one. Whoever it is going through a lot to disguise his voice."

"I am on edge Boss Lady. We should call Anthony or Stephen to make a police report."

"Girl fix your face and meet me in the office."

Thinking to myself, "*If I call them, it will be after I speak to Shafiq.*"

She comes with bloodshot eyes as I finish the detailed conversation and says, "I am calling Anthony."

"Bullshit, we can file a report at the station and have lunch."

"Okay Boss Lady, I will be your chauffeur for the day," she wipes her eyes and smiles with her keys dangling.

She drives a *2016 Fully Loaded Deep Impact Blue Ford Mustang GT 2-Door Convertible*. I mean this bitch is S.W.E.E.T to the depth of her honeycomb.

Luckily for me the ride to the station is a few minutes because I have a migraine from her rambling.

She speaks to an officer at the desk while I sit to the side observing the overall commotion.

One catches my attention. A brown skinned female, short natural hair, average features with a nice moon pie ass, crying to a male officer about being abused.

He asks, "Ma'am, I need for you to calm down. What is your husband's name?"

She responds while looking around, "Detective Stephen Chambers."

He snatches her by the arm and mumbles, "You are asking for trouble."

She talks to herself a few chairs from me and gives a loud sigh.

Did she say she is married to Detective Stephen Chambers?

Through every Stormy Cloud a Rainbow Appears...

Fifteen minutes passed and Bianca returns with a snapping turtle attitude explaining how she filed a worthless complaint.

"There ain't enough evidence. If anything, else happens, come back and make another report."

"What the fuck? I guess we have to wait until he puts his hands on you for them to get off their asses."

The young lady chimes in, "As long as it is not one of *New Orleans Finest*, then you might have a chance."

Bianca points at her and whispers, "Who is fucking talking to her?"

I shush her, spin around to the young lady and say, "We are going to lunch and you are more than welcome to join us. By the way, my name is Alexis and this is my best friend Bianca."

She speaks through tears, "Thank you so much. I would like that. My name is Rachael."

"Hey Rachael, it is nice to meet you. We will see you at *Acme Oyster House* in 15 minutes."

Bianca snatches my arm and blurts, "Boss Lady, what the fuck are you up to?"

"My mind is always on something and it is better when shit falls in my lap."

Bianca and I drive in silence. We arrive moments later and seat at my favorite table. I order a dozen of *Chargrilled Oysters*, three *Acme Poopa*, three *New Orleans Bread Pudding with Whiskey Sauce* and shots of *Patron* and *Acme Sunset.*

She nervously arrives as the waiter brings our drinks. It takes two rounds of *Patron* to take control of Rachael's tongue when she admits, "My husband and I have been married for less than a year and would have never thought he would hit me."

"What are you going to do?" Bianca asks reaching for a napkin.

"I don't know. All of the women I dated never treated me like this."

My food stops in my throat but interjects, "What happened to your face? If you don't mind me asking."

"He came home irate from work. I don't remember why we were arguing but he slapped me. After a few hours of trying to calm him down he shouted he would kill me. He followed me out of the room, picked up a kitchen chair, and hit across my face. I ran to the neighbor's house and they saw several bruises on my face and arms; they called the police. When the officers asked, who caused the injuries and I said his name. They wouldn't do a report and left."

"Has he ever given you signs of control or abuse before you married him?" I ask.

"Honestly, I only knew him three months before we got married. And what makes it worse…"

"Don't worry Rachael, you have friends now. You don't have to say anything else." Bianca announces with a hug.

"Yeah Rachael, good fortune has come your way." I suggest adding to their hugs.

Revenge is sweeter when its finger licking good…

3191

Chapter 5

The ride to the office is joyful as the music blast through the speakers. She points to me and we sing, "*Prepared*" by *Jill Scott*. Angelic and demonic whispers flow though my membranes as she parks.

I contemplated on shattering dreams and demolishing bridges since my sentencing. Listening to these words, I am excited about making them a reality. Fantasizing the smell of someone's demise, I didn't realize I am in my office. Green rose petals on the floor leading to my desk and 14 long stemmed ones spread across with a card reading,

"Happy 14-month anniversary My Love.
You are the moon that shines throughout the darkness
The Sun who brightens the clouds
Your presence awakens my spirit
And absence rattles my mental
Never afraid to say I enjoy the flutter of butterflies and galloping of unicorns
Looking to spend many more.
Shafiq"

"FUCK! I forgot." I yell digging through my purse for my cell.

Phone rings, rings, rings…... I hang up.

Walk to the front by Bianca, "Hey, whatever happened the other night?"

"Oh yeah, I knew it was something I forgot to tell you. Veronica left early and I had to reschedule one of my appointments."

"Long story short, she came to the house with information about Clarissa. Detective told her they found her purse and belongings."

"She left work and rushed to your house for that bullshit; she could have called you."

"It's okay Bianca. I understand she is concerned and I would be too if I gave a fuck but I don't. As an employer, I will do whatever is necessary to find her but that is it."

Glance at my phone and no missed call. What the hell is Shafiq doing?

Oh well; scroll through my contacts and send a text to Frederick, "Hit me up," as I head to my office.

"Hey Tweety, on my way to a meeting. How about lunch tomorrow at *Lil Dizzy's Café* at 12pm?" He responds.

"Okay, your treat."

"Of course, it's not like you aren't good for it."

"Whatever, go to your meeting. See you tomorrow," I reply looking at the petals on the floor.

Bianca comes in with a huge FedEx box and says, "Special Delivery."

"For me?" Taking the package from her.

"What the hell happened in here?"

"Girl who else but Shafiq."

We look at each other, smile and clean the office.

Bianca expresses, "I am happy for you. He seems to bring out more than a twinkle."

"I have trust issues but I know he is my soulmate; I can't see myself with no one but him."

"I know what you mean. One day I will find someone to make me happy until then I have to do something with these damn petals," laughing out the door.

Sit in my chair, tear the box and stare for a few minutes. Gather my thoughts and remove the soft cotton drawstring bag.

I am teary-eyed pulling out a *Duxbury Weekender Toasted Almond Melbourne Brahmin Handbag* with matching *Debra Wallet.*

I love nice things but this is too much.

Call his phone again but no answer.

Bianca walks in, sees the gifts and screams, "OH MY GOODNESS BOSS LADY!!!!!!"

"Girl, be quiet."

"Oh, I have a gift for you."

She runs and comes back with a gorgeous frosted glass bowl with green rose petals floating in water and a 22-oz. jar of *Yankee Candle Cucumber Melon* in the middle.

"Aww, this is beautiful. Thank you, Bianca."

"Anything for you Boss Lady."

"I am going home. Better yet, you and the rest of the staff enjoy your day off tomorrow. Oh yeah, tell Tyrone sexy ass he is free to go also."

"Huh?"

"You heard me. I have to get prepared remember."

The ride to the condo felt like I was riding on the clouds in heaven. I cradle my gifts, rush through the door, drop the briefcase on the sofa and inhale the smell of peppermint in the air.

Slowly humming the tune to the bedroom and a *Kendall + Kylie Poppy Red Sleeveless Pleated Bodice Dress* with

Christian Louboutin Leopard Print Red Sole Pumps and *Matching Purse* lies on the bed.

A card on top of the *Neiman Marcus* shopping bag reads,

"*Landry's Seafood Restaurant at 8pm. Don't be late.*"

I don't know what to do with this man. I am not used to this attention but I truly appreciate the gesture.

Looking at the time, "Damn, it's 5:30. I better hurry."

Shower, lotion and spray in his favorite *Black Currant Vanilla* from *Bath and Body Works*. Lightly apply enough makeup to ensure his lips lick twice on sight.

Slide in the dress and realizes he didn't buy panties; I won't wear any. Turn sideways in the mirror and admire the frame smiling back.

Time check – 6:47…. late for real…

Switch purses and head out the door. Luckily the drive is ten minutes away but the restaurant is packed. Cruising the area a few times to waste fifteen minutes. Nervous as I parallel park and see a waiter standing by his car with a sign "*Alexis Roulle.*"

Shafiq parked by the *Historic Canal Lighthouse* and not a pleasant walk in heels.

I turn the ignition off, open the door and cross both legs before leaving the driver side.

The waiter looks, smiles and says, "You must be Ms. Roulle."

"What gave it away?"

"The shoes and the eyes. Ms. Roulle, my name is Le`mone. I will take you to your date but I have been instructed to blindfold you."

"Blindfold me? What the fuck is going on?"

"Ma'am, I assure you, it is no funny stuff."

"If it is, I am coming back and fucking you up Le`mone."

"Yes ma'am."

He helps me on the golf cart and blindfolds me.

I am sure he is driving in a circle.

I sniff the air and ask. "Is that water?"

No response……

My mind wonders to the worst and they are going to kill me. He bought me all the way out here to bury me.

What kind of man have I fallen in love with?

Someone grabs my hand minutes later and helps me down. I stand in silence with the wind.

"Hello? Hello? Shafiq?"

Nothing.

"Shafiq?" SHAFIQ!" Taking two steps to the left.

Still nothing.

"Stop fucking playing, this shit is not funny!" I yell.

A soft kiss hits my neck sending an orgasmic shock.

The blindfold is undone afterwards grabbing both wrists with force.

What the fuck is going on?

My vision becoming clearer of a 70-ft. yacht standing tall among the blue waters by the pier.

He releases my wrists.

I turn around to hug him but….

He is on one knee and pleads, “Alexis, would you marry me?”

I feel stoned. I can’t move my feet and my mouth is numb.

“Alexis, Alexis.” Calling and getting up from his knees.

I feel someone shaking my shoulders and I utter, “Uh.”

“Alexis, did you hear me?”

“I am sorry. I thought you asked me to marry you.”

“Alex, I did.”

The crowds stop eating and stand over the balcony as they hear the ruckus and proposal.

Shafiq blurts, “The boat staff is waiting to reveal her name. Yes, or No?”

“Of course, I will marry you.”

He spins around and yells, “She says YES!”

The crew releases her name. We run on board, enjoy our dinner and the rest of the evening is….

CREOLISTIC…

Chapter 6
(Anthony)

"Man, I don't know the last time you came to my crib to chill," says Anthony drinking a *Red Stripe*.

"I had to get the hell out of the house. I can't watch the *Lakers and Jazz* game in peace. She is getting on my fucking nerves," responds Stephen with his head in the refrigerator.

"Sit down and watch the last few minutes."

"Damn, *Kobe Bryant* is showing his ass off."

Ringtone of *Darling Nikki* plays interrupting my attention from Kobe's scoring 47 points.

"What the fuck nigga, silence dat shit," I yell.

"I am tired of this motherfucka nagging me. I ain't talking to her," Stephen responds.

The excitement of the game has us on our feet as history is made in front of our eyes.

Ringtone comes on again. I put my face in my hand, look away from the TV and within seconds the commentator announces Kobe has scored 60 points. Snatch the phone out of his hands and sling it across the room.

"Didn't I tell you to put dat bitch on vibrate," saying in disgust.

"What the fuck Anthony. You need to control your temper," yelling and walking to the phone.

"I missed the rest of the game fucking with you and her dumb ass. This was *Kobe Bryant* last game after 20 years with the *Los Angeles Lakers*. I shouldn't watch the fucking highlights *on ESPN*, if I was watching the fucking game." screaming and throwing *Doritos*.

He gets the broom, cleans up the mess and inspects the phone, "You broke it."

"You got a *Samsung Galaxy 7*; you better have insurance."

"When you were in college, did you have a temper?" Stephen asks.

"What kind of question is that? You should have asked did you wear boxers or briefs. Sometimes, I wonder why we are boys."

Stephen answers jokily, "I ask myself the same thing."

"No, only thing I did was baseball and books."

"You didn't pledge or party."

"Naw, all my free time was spent with Brittany. I used to pound her pussy after class then slide in her ass for lunch."

"Wow, you never mentioned her before."

"Nigga, Brittany was my bitch for two years. White chick, blonde hair, perky titties and an ass made for spanking. I loved stroking dat tight pussy and she took all of this dick."

"Go ahead with dat shit, you are getting excited over there."

"Hell yeah, it's the only reason Bianca caught my eye because of all of the shit Brittany did," licking my lips and grabbing my pants.

"What happened to her?" Stephen asks

"The fucking pump stopped working."

Stephen looks at me sideways and laughs.

I couldn't help it so I burst out and say, "I ain't shame."

An hour later of bullshitting, eating and drinking, my phone rings.

"Hello."

"Hey Anthony, this is Lawrence."

"Hey Lawrence, what's up? Do I need to come in?"

"Naw nothing like that. I have been trying to call Stephen and can't get through."

"His ass is right here," passing the phone.

Putting him on speakerphone, "What's going on?" Still trying to get his phone to work.

"It's personal." He replies.

"No problem, what's up?" Stephen answers worriedly.

"Yesterday a brown skinned chick came to the precinct and wanted to make a report."

"And?"

"She said she was your wife and wanted to file a domestic assault report."

"THAT BITCH!" Stephen yells.

"Damn bruh." I respond.

"I told her to seriously think about the charges then she left. No one knows about this. Handle it before it bites you on the ass. Do you hear me Detective?" Lawrence scolds.

"I hear you loud and clear Lieutenant."

We end the conversation and Stephen looks at me with fury.

"Calm down, I will talk to her." I answer throwing another beer.

LCP

Chapter 7
(Alexis)

Waking up to the leftover fresh water smell with Shafiq is a fairytale. We sailed on *Lake Ponchatrain* throughout the night before returning home. I am always treated like a queen and looking forward to being a wife. Sooner or later he should come from the shadows.

Death of a musical genius interrupts my concentration. The legacy and vitality of *Prince* forever remains. Scrambling through my CD collection and play *Diamonds and Pearls*. Sit on the sofa, feet on the coffee table and the words hits me instantly with a tear,

"This will be the day
That you will hear me say
That I will never run away

I am here for you
Love is meant for two
Now tell me what you're gonna do

If I gave you diamonds and pearls
Would you be a happy boy or a girl
If I could I would give you the world
But all I can do is just offer you my love"

I guess for the first time in my life, I can truly say I am in love but I have egos to destroy. Leave the living room to pick my style for the day. Ummm, let's do sporty.

I lay out an *Olive Side Fringe Tank, White Mid-Rise Linen Cropped Wide Leg Pants* from *Old Navy* and pair of *Olive Anne Klein Loafers*.

Singing *Sexy M.F.* in the kitchen and make a cup of *Chai Tea Latte* with *Land-o Lakes Half and Half* and a shot of *Grand Marnier.* I don't know why I have this concoction but it vitalizes my day.

The clock on the wall displays 9:30 am; I can take my time. Lounge around, turn off the music and an episode of *Forensic Files* gets my full attention.

I won't tell you which one however the details will be revised in an upcoming "accident."

Damn, I lost track of time; jump up and dress.

Phone rings, "Hello."

"Hello My Love," Shafiq answers.

"Hey behbee. What happened to my ride this morning?"

"Alexis, you have a lifetime of saddling." He responds with laughter.

"I have a lunch meeting at 12pm. What's on your agenda?"

"You know me."

"Hunting huh?"

"Oh yeah, surprises come to the patient. Call me when you finish. Eye love u."

"Love you too," I reply hanging up.

Jump in the truck to meet Frederick at *Lil Dizzy's Café*. I drive down *Esplanade Avenue* and shocked I haven't explored my beautiful city like I should. Besides if I am in the market to dump a body, I need to know the depth of my surroundings.

I park on the street, walk in and Frederick looks edible sitting at the table.

He meets me halfway and greets with a hug, "Hey Tweety, I mean Ms. Roulle."

"You are the only one who can say it."

He pulls out my chair and announces, "You are going to love the food."

"I never been here and I am hungry."

The waitress tiptoes to table, "Good afternoon, your food will be out in a minute." Placing two sweet teas and napkins.

"Freddie, you don't know what I want to eat."

"I got what I wanted in your mouth…hush. Anyway, what's up? Wait, don't tell me, you ready to give me that pussy!"

"The hell Freddie. Stop! I need a job done. Name your price."

"How big?"

"$10,000 worth but I can't afford any fuck ups. I need it done in three days. Can you do it?

"Tweety, your dominance makes my dick hard. Shit, anything for you but I have a separate request for my payment."

Our food arrives and I have the *Strip Steak, Baked Macaroni and Cheese* with *Collard Greens* and *Bread Pudding*. He has *Gumbo, Fried Chicken* and *Green Beans*.

Gazing at the smorgasbord then my stomach and say, "Guess I will work it off later."

"Same ole Alexis."

We enjoy lunch and discuss phase one. An hour later my phone rings.

Peek at it in disgust but answers, "Hey Veronica."

"Can you take care of my dog?"

"Sure. What's wrong?

Her voice trembles with tears, "I miss her and going to find her."

"Look for who? Have you been drinking?"

"I am tired and only want to talk to her. I don't know why Clarissa left without telling me."

"Veronica, let me finish my meeting. I will come see you."

She speaks through hysterical cries but I am unable to make it out and the phone goes dead.

"Fuck!" I express gobbling down the sweet tea. "I gotta go Freddie. Call me later."

I hurriedly scramble my things and jump in the truck.

This motherfucka is getting on my damn last nerves.

Pound my fist on the steering wheel, turn on the ignition and speed to her house. It usually takes 45 minutes but I make it in 30 without a police escort.

Beat on the door for a while but no answer.

Call her phone. No answer

Break the living room window, climb in and hear the music blasting.

Shout her name through the noise until I turn it off, "Veronica? Veronica?"

Run to the bedroom and find her with a pill bottle hanging out of her hand with an empty can of *Budd Light Mixx Tail Long Island Iced Tea* on the nightstand.

"What the fuck Veronica?" I yell holding her.

Slap her a few times, check her pulse and call 911.

"Why would you do something crazy like this? Get up Veronica, please wake up."

Time seem to move slow as I hear pounding at the door.

Gently lay her down, open the door for EMT and explain how I found her.

Tech says, "Ma'am, calm down and have a seat over there. We will do everything we can."

"Whatever you must do, please do it." I respond.

Seconds later they strap her to the gurney and explains, "Ma'am, we are taking her to *East Jefferson General Hospital*. You can ride with us or meet us there."

"Is she going to be okay?"

"I am so sorry but she has expired."

I stand in disbelief, compose myself and call Shafiq and Bianca.

Thread is unravelling and time for exposure.

Chapter 8
(Veronica)

Bianca paces the emergency waiting room floor as I walk in.

One of the paramedics take her body out of the ambulance and says, "We have paperwork to do. Have a seat, I will come back to get you."

"I apologize but I didn't get your first name."

"It's okay ma'am. My name is Adonis."

"Adonis, thank you so much. I am Alexis and this is my best friend Bianca."

"Nice to meet you. I will return shortly." He responds down the hall with Veronica on the gurney.

"Boss Lady, what happened?" Bianca asks.

"She took the whole bottle of *Valium*. I can't believe she let Clarissa drive her to do this. It doesn't make sense."

"Did she leave a note?"

"Shit, I didn't look. I was concerned about getting help. Tomorrow we can check and pack her things."

"Okay, I'll call everyone and arrange a meeting."

Adonis walks down the hall, sits next to me and says, "Ms. Alexis, the coroner won't let you see her unless you are family."

"Bullshit."

He lightly squeezes my knee and says, "Calm down. They should contact her next of kin. Do you have any information?"

"She hasn't spoken to them in over 10 years. This is straight bullshit. I am calling the Chief."

"Chief?"

"Yeah the Chief of Police."

"No need."

Still sitting in disbelief. This is a serious setback for my plans but now my tongue craves blood.

He returns minutes later and says, "My supervisor will be out in a minute."

The other paramedic comes down the hallway, gives him a nod and walks out.

Adonis leans and whispers in my ear, "I finally meet Ms. Roulle."

I quickly turn with brows up and responds, "Huh?"

He kisses my right cheek, slides a piece of paper in my hand and says, "We can be great service to each other. Call me," and walks away.

A bald, caramel, slender but tone man. I couldn't let him know when he touched my knee it sent fireworks throughout my body.

I open my hand and think out loud, "I need a man in the mix."

Bianca stands in from of me and snaps, "Boss Lady, stop thinking business."

Throw the number in my purse and answers, "You are correct. Did you call everyone?"

"Yes, the meeting is tomorrow at 9 am."

"It is late; I will see you in the morning."

"We will get through this."

She gives me a big hug. Her phone rings and she leaves.

Taking a deep breath, get up and head to the parking lot.

A shadow comes towards me saying, "Alex, as soon as I got your message, I came straight over."

"Where the fuck was you?"

"I can't share it right now but whatever I was doing it is for you. What the hell happened and lower your damn voice."

We continue walking to my truck as I explain everything. Instantly a smirk appears on his face.

"Behbee, it is not funny."

"Not funny but ironic."

"What the hell does that supposed to mean?"

"Meaning My Love, it's time to get rid of Clarissa."

"Shafiq, I have plans for her disposal; focus on this first. Okay?"

"Okay My Love, I will follow your lead."

"Better yet, since you are here. Let's go to Veronica's house and see what we can find."

"I am down."

We race to her house and scramble through its entirety. She must have been on a diet since the cabinets and refrigerator were bare.

Was she getting prepared?

She appeared peaceful when I found her. I assume her pain was no longer a factor.

We search through her drawers, closets and shoe boxes and find absolutely nothing.

"Bae, she didn't leave a clue or anything."

"Alex, one thing women cherish more than clothes are pictures. Where is her phone?"

I immediately find her phone and cash box between the bed and nightstand. I place them on the pillow and give Shafiq a confused look.

"Alex, sit down. I will open it."

He unlocks it, scrolls and mumbles, "What the fuck?"

I respond, "Is it bad? Please tell me it is not bad?'

"No, it is not bad; it's fucked up."

He slides the phone and says, "Swipe about 15 times."

My hand trembles as I place my left index finger on the arrow. I quickly go from having sympathy for her to wanting to resurrect and kill her again.

As I see the hurtful evidence, Shafiq opens the cash box, dumps it on the bed and walks away. "Alex, you have 20 minutes to absorb everything."

I lift my head with the phone in one hand and photos in the other as tears take over my vision. Searching through find several letters to and from Clarissa.

Shafiq leaves the house and return with a small plastic bag and demands, "Whatever you want to keep from that no-good bitch put it in here and the rest I will take care of."

Wiping my face, I say softly, "She was having threesomes with Clarissa and Stephen. Behbee, did you hear me? That bitch was fucking him too."

"I heard you My Love but it is time to go."

After sending three pictures to my email, I read one of the letters dated a year ago,

Clarissa,

I can't share you any longer. Leave him alone! If Alexis gets wind of this, we will be floating in the canal. He doesn't love you like I do. Please reconsider so we can start over.

I gaze at Shafiq, "You mean to tell me Veronica killed herself over Clarissa. Both of those bitches deserves to be with each other."

Helping me up to walk out the house, he says, "Yes they do."

"Behbee, I am going to be sick." Feels like my feet hit the pavement a thousand times.

He interrupts and blurts, "Fuck, I forgot something in the house."

I stumble to the truck and vomit at the front passenger tire.

I can't believe this shit, every woman claiming to be my friend over the years has crossed me. Why?

He hugs my waist, cleans my face and says, "This is the perfect time to relax."

"I can't relax. I think I am having a damn heart attack."

He opens the door and drives across the street to the vacant lot.

"I promise everything will work out how it is destined. Trust me." He says rolling a thick blunt from his bag.

"Shafiq, take me home. I have had enough for the day."

"Not yet My Love. A sparkle will appear to make you feel better in 3.2.1."

He passes the blunt, I take a deep pull and enjoy the red shadowing the moon.

"This is a beautiful sight. Thank you Shafiq."

"Happy to make you smile My Love."

Shitty things are purged through flames....

Chapter 9
(Anthony)

Taking a break from patrolling the avenue. I pull over to enjoy a quick bite.

I don't need anything to stir my plans.

Ten minute passes and a call interrupts my relaxation, "Hey, I was thinking about you?"

A voice answers, "Really? Do you have a few minutes to talk?"

"Sure, what's up?"

"I don't have any friends but you." The voice says while holding back tears.

"Rachael, you can tell me anything. I am listening."

"Stephen hit me."

"You are kidding, right?"

"No, I am not. I am pressing charges tomorrow."

Damn I need to think of something quick.

"Wait, think about what it would do to him!!"

"Anthony, he didn't think of me when he threw the chair."

"This is bullshit. I will talk to him, okay?"

"He doesn't want to be married. He is cheating on me."

"Girl, you are smoking that shit. He works too much for someone else."

"Fuck his hours and him. I know what the hell my gut tells me."

"You know you can trust me. When he comes home tonight, I promise he will have a better attitude. You are like a sister to me. I got you."

"I hope so because I don't trust his conniving ass. I appreciate you for listening."

"No problem."

We end the call and I need to come up with a way to approach him with this damn nonsense. I told him to get rid of her a long time ago.

Reach for my food, take a bite and throw it against the window, "Fuck, talking to that bitch got my food cold."

Tapping noise on the driver's window changes my concentration. Roll the window down and asks, "What's up?"

Officer answers, "I came over to make sure you were okay."

"And you are?"

"I am your new partner, Officer Jones." He answers reaching out his hand.

"Well Officer, the first thing to learn is never walk up on anyone without probable cause."

Snatch him inside the window. I grab his Taser and discharge it to his upper shoulder. He fights to break free but I hit his hip area just below the rib cage. The electrical impulses cause his body to have uncontrollable muscle contractions. I mush his forehead and he falls to the ground.

I jump out the car, stand over his body and whispers, "No one interrupts my fucking lunch."

Drops the Taser next to his body, kicks his face and snort a little bit as soon as I get in the car.

"Whew! What a fucking rush!!!" I shout wiping the residue off my noise.

Dial 911 from my throw away phone, "Where is your emergency?"

"Uh, I'm on *North Broad Street* and *Bienville*."

"What is the emergency?"

"Two white guys assaulted a police officer."

"Sir, we have dispatched two patrol cars, please stay at the scene until they arrive."

"Yeah right."

"Excuse me Sir," the dispatch snaps.

I disconnect the call, finish my cold sandwich, and pull off. Glance in the rearview mirror and laughs at Officer Jones' body still twitching.

Stephen better not told that fuck nigga where I hang. I couldn't jeopardize anything. It was him or me.

Drive back to the precinct and head to the property room.

"Hey Dennis, I got some shit to log in."

"Detective you know the procedure." Getting up from his desk and places the log book with bags on the counter.

"Man, I am happy this crazy day is over."

"Mine started two hours ago." He says analyzing the written information.

I waste a little time with small talk and put the property in an evidence bag. Write my name, identification number, contents and initials then seal.

"Damn, three pounds of cocaine. You in narcotics now?"

"Naw, caught some niggas on the corner up to no good."

Dennis records the information on a paper sack, drops the bag inside and says while pointing for my initials, "I hear ya. We got to keep that shit off the streets. I wish a lot of cops did things out of their division to keep that poison away."

"I am only doing what comes natural. Enjoy your shift."

I take a shortcut through the precinct for Stephen but instead hear a few officers talking about an attack on one of our own.

On my way to the exit, another officer stops me and asks, "Hey Anthony, did you hear what happened to Officer Jones."

I reply, "Who is Officer Jones?"

"You haven't met him? He is your new partner."

"I have a new partner, damn. When was someone going to fucking tell me?"

Lieutenant comes out and yells, "Detective, my office, now!"

I shrug to the officer and say, "Guess I am getting briefed."

Speed walk to his door and announces with a salute, "Reporting for duty."

"Come in and close the door."

"What did I do this time?" I ask sitting down.

"Thank goodness it's not you. I put Stephen on administrative leave until we can clear up the domestic assault charge."

"I thought you said that a report wasn't given."

"Yeah, I did but her neighbors made the report since the officers on call refused. Now, I have three people on leave for bullshit."

"Fuck!!!"

"You are right about that shit. I am assigning you another partner."

"Maybe it is best I take a week off to talk to him."

He sits with hands above the headrest and declares, "That is a good idea. The robbery division is slow. When do you want to start?"

"Immediately if I can."

"No problem, fill out the request and I will approve it."

"I heard something about Officer Jones. What the hell happened?"

"He was attacked behind the old *Schwegmann*."

"Why was he over there? Was it a code 65?"

"Only thing I know was an anonymous call came through about a solicitation and officer was hurt. I am waiting to clear everything on my desk and head to the hospital."

"Okay, give me a few to fill out the request." I say hurriedly to my desk.

Log on the computer, fill out the paperwork and print. As I get up for the copier, my phone rings. I press ignore without checking the caller.

Snatching the leave request, head to the Lieutenant's office and my phone rings again.

"Someone really wants to talk to you." He says jokingly approving my mini vacation.

"I hope it's wet pussy."

He laughs and replies, "Enjoy your leave Anthony. Get your crazy ass out of my office."

I examine several missed calls and think, "What has happened now?"

Run to my car, call the number and say with an attitude, "What the fuck is it?"

"Hey, this is Tyrone. We need a drop off at the *Joliet Street* spot.

"Okay I am on my way."

Hang up, scoop my finger in the bag on the passenger side floor, rub it on my teeth and hit *I-10.*

Courage comes in a liquid and a powder…

Chapter 10
(Adonis)

Sitting on the floor reminiscing of how many of my friends claim to be 100. When I was locked up, they diminished or showed their true colors. Like those old folks used to say if you knew they were snakes to others what makes you special never to get bitten.

Clasp the phone in my hand, take a deep breath and call Frederick, "Good morning Handsome."

"Good morning Tweety," he replies with laughter.

"I will make it quick, is everything in place?"

"Damn, straight to business. Plan is together just waiting on your word."

"That is what I like to hear. Call you around 8pm with all the details. Cool?"

"Tweety, you know I got you."

After we hang up, Shafiq walks in looking sexy as fuck.

He greets me by holding my head and passionately kisses.

"Hey My Love."

I answer fighting goosebumps over my body, "Hey my Behbee."

I stand, hug his neck and whispers, "I miss you."

"How much?"

Sashay across the room and lock my door. As I twist my ass back in his direction, unbutton my blouse showing the *Red/Black Front Shelf Bra* accentuating my cleavage.

Place his face between my titties and mention, "You want them."

He plops me on the desk and notices the garter belt.

I open my legs wide displaying the wetness on the matching *Red/Black Satin and cinched lace front with bow* from *Frederick's of Hollywood.*

He licks his finger, trace the outline of my drips and taste the tip. I grip the side of the desk, slide to the edge with one knee touching my face. His tongue tiptoes across my panties and circles my clitoris in an S-shape.

The fluttering of his pink tingles my entire body. He slides the fabric to the side, inserts a finger in my pussy and the more I try not to moan he slurps harder.

I think he is sketching his name on my pear stem, S-H-A-F, I can't hold it.

"Ummmmm, shit…stop." I finally let out.

Slowing tracing from the top of my mound to my valley. I swear I hear boots splashing in water but it's my ocean in high tide. I clench my jaws, tightly clench the desk and explode in his mouth.

He penetrates my ass with his nails, tips me over his mouth like a teapot drinking every drop.

He comes up, licks my lips and utters, "You are so sweet," while massaging my erect areoles.

Shafiq unlocks the door as I get myself together. Walks back over and slides his hands over his hard missile, "He misses you."

I open his pants and he moves my hand and says, "Later My Love, only came for a quick brunch."

"You denying me?"

Before he says anything, Bianca comes in and interrupts, "Hey Boss Lady, someone is here to see you."

Turn my attention to her and add, “I don’t have an appointment today. Who is it?”

“It’s the paramedic from the other night. Don’t forget we have a meeting with everyone in an hour.”

“Shit, my mind was on other things,” looking at Shafiq.

“I apologize, hey Boss Man,” she says with flustered cheeks.

“What’s up Bianca,” he answers with a smile.

“Bring him to my office to see what he wants.”

She jets down the hallway and Shafiq says, “That’s my cue, I will see you tonight.”

“No Behbee, I want you here,” holding his hand.

“Okay.”

Bianca returns with Adonis and I say bluntly as he walks in, “Rule number one, never come to my office unless you have an appointment. Are we fucking clear?”

He looks at Shafiq standing behind me and replies, “Loud and clear.”

“Good. How may I help you?”

“I want to be a ThrillPleaser.”

Shafiq and I respond with laughter.

“I don’t think you can handle what the clients pay for.”

“They don’t call me Da Don for nothing. Do I need an interview because I am ready? Since you are the head bitch, I will show you what I am capable of.”

Shafiq makes a step and I slowly move him back. “Being the head bitch as you call it comes with perks and that is not one of them.”

“He is so confident, I want to see this play out,” Shafiq blurts out.

I give him a confused look, “Huh?”

He has never been involved in approving my people and doing a terrible job.

I call Bianca and asks, “How many are here for the meeting?”

“We have five.”

“Good, can you bring LaToya?”

She hangs up and returns ten minutes later.

They march in with perplexed expressions and inquire, “Boss Lady, is something wrong?”

I turn and respond with LaToya code name, “TNT, everything is good. I need you for an interview. That’s all. Bianca, start the meeting and be there soon.”

“Take your time, I got it under control.”

She winks and closes the door.

“This little interview will get you off your probation and on the real shit. Get as comfortable as you want. Da Don says he is ready to be a ThrillPleaser and you will be his tester.”

“Hell yeah, I am ready.” She states taking off her yoga pants and laying on the sofa.

Adonis glances at me and remarks, “This will be quick and easy.”

I shake my head and convey, “You have fifteen minutes Da Don.”

His face disappears between her legs and periodically peeks at me for approval. Unfortunately, I know nothing except a poker face.

Hearing the lap licks cause my pussy to twitch, looking back at Shafiq and he is turned on.

Seven minutes later, she makes soft sounds. Turn to Shafiq again, he slowly goes up and down on his shaft. The more he looks at them, they faster he cups his manhood.

I kneel waiting for my treat and hum, "Give mama her cream Behbee."

Five minutes afterwards she yells, "Fuck, I'm cumming."

He whispers, "Me too."

I part my lips and welcome his scrumptious load. Tasting all the fruits he loves.

Shafiq states as he helps me up, "My Love, I am so sorry. I don't know what came over me."

"This time was an excuse." I reply wiping my mouth.

"TNT, you okay over there?"

She exhales and moans, "I'm wonderful."

I crawl to the sofa as Shafiq stands in disbelief, touch Adonis' shoulder and reveal, "You were pushing it but awesome job. Welcome to Majestic Pleasures."

I love knowing everyone's fetish....

Faith

Chapter 11
(Alexis)

After our interesting lunch session, LaToya, Adonis and I walk in the conference room as Bianca tells everyone about the death of Veronica.

"Hey Boss Lady, you can take over."

"It's okay, please continue." I answer sitting in the corner with legs crossed.

LaToya and Adonis blend in with the rest of the ladies at the conference table.

"The disappearance of Clarissa and the death of Veronica have left a hole in our heart," Bianca states.

Mercedes interrupts and asks, "Is our safety in jeopardy?"

Tigri responds, "Fuck safety, I am worried about my money."

A commotion stirs and Bianca loses control of the meeting.

I stand, clear my throat and say, "Enough of the bullshit. Everything has been taken care of for Veronica and her family. As far as Clarissa, don't know and truly don't fucking care."

Silence hits the room with blank stares.

"We have a new member of Majestic Pleasures, Adonis please stand."

He rises to his feet and grips his dick, "Good afternoon ladies," and sits down.

"As ya'll can tell he has no shame however we will train the puppy to become a true dog."

Cassandra interjects while licking her lips, “I need some of that in my life.”

Adonis answers, “I got a lot to put between them.”

I slap my hand on the table and roar, “There will be no fucking among the team.”

I pinch each ThrillPleasers like grandma used to do around the table. “Now, that I have everyone’s attention. A private Masquerade Party is in the plans for Saturday evening. Bianca has sent the emails to the VIPs and prospective members.

Mercedes responds, “About time we have real fun.”

“If you put that camera down you could have a lot more.” I answer sarcastically.

The room fills with laughter and suggestions.

“Bianca, make sure Adonis fills out the paperwork correctly. Remember everyone, this is one of many events. If you want to invite your client do it. However, be prepared for new meat. Are there any questions?”

Chanae` stands and admits, “Fucking on the water, I can’t wait.”

I shake my head as they discuss the attire.

Bianca answers the vibrating phone as she walks to her desk with Adonis following her scent. “Stop calling my damn phone.” She yells.

“Ladies pardon the interruptions.” I dismiss the group and trail Bianca to her desk.

“What is going on?”

Adonis says jokingly, “Guess that type of shit happens when you got that snapper.”

“Shut the hell up and finish your paperwork,” I respond.

"Bianca, are you okay?"

"No, the calls are starting again. I don't know who it is or why."

"Did he say anything?"

"He was moaning then he said get on your knees and get this nut bitch."

"Can you recognize anything about his voice?"

"Don't you think I would tell you?" She discloses with anger.

"Calm the fuck down. I am trying to help." I reply abruptly.

Adonis breaks his silence, "How about narrowing it down to the people with your number?"

"I tried that and only nine people have my number and none of them are men."

He continues, "Okay? To me, someone is really trying to get your attention even if it is the wrong kind; I'm just saying." He puts his head back into the document.

Bianca answers, "I don't have a clue."

She puts her hand over her face and cries.

I answer, "Get it together. Leave your personal shit out of the door and do your job."

I stomp the linoleum on the way to my office and slam the door.

I must find out who Mr. Telephone Man is before I knock her head off.

Work waits for no one and it is damn near 3:30 pm. Check three voice messages and one from Mrs. Fountaine.

Good afternoon Ms Roulle,

How is the paperwork coming along? My husband and I are looking forward to a little sexual exhibition. It has been a long time since I have gotten fucked until I puke. Our sex life has become mundane and we are screaming for adventure. I wouldn't mind tasting some of your juicy pussy also. Looking forward to doing a little bit of anything. Call my cell.

Toodles,
Carmen

Well, Well, Well…The mouse wants to play with Big Kitty huh?

Call Shafiq from the office phone, "Hey Behbee, what cha doing?"

He replies with laughter, "The usual hunting. What's up?"

"Oh nothing. I was thinking that we didn't finish our meal."

"Really My Love? Where do you want to go?"

"My office in two hours and the menu is sweet pussy."

"See you then."

A smile comes across my face when we hang up.

I send an email to Bianca to go home and relax. I will lock up.

I am in no mood to see her face or hear her voice. All I want is dick.

After she leaves, I go to my car and get my workout bag. Unfortunately, I haven't been able to go to the gym but Shafiq gives all the muscle failure I need.

While in my office, I light the candle, rummage through my bag for body wash, lotion, and towel. Collect everything and head to my office shower.

Thirty minutes later, I come out the bathroom completely refreshed and go down the corridors of the bookstore.

I think I want to fuck in the Romantic Room.

Run back to my office, snatch the candle, and bring it to the room. On the way out, I leave a note on the door.

Tasting in Room 2

Turn on *Avant,* lie on the bed with towel wrapped around my body and wait.

Unsure of how long I dozed off but awaken by sucking sounds between my legs.

I jump up and Shafiq whispers, "My Sleeping Beauty is up."

I hurriedly unbutton his pants and divulge, "Leave your boots on."

He softly kisses my earlobe, turn me around and throw me on the bed.

He cuffs my waist, lift me on my knees and utters, "Is this is what you want?"

"Yes."

His inches grow in my uterus with each thrust.

He drags my body to the edge of the bed. Lifts my leg and bangs my pussy with his left hook hitting my spot.

He pulls out and sucks my sweetness like a child with a sugarcane. Fingers my pussy until she speaks her own language for his mouth.

I grasp the sheets and scream, "OH MY FUCKING GOODNESS!!!!!!

His mouth covers my fruit with the fluttering of his tongue until my right leg shakes.

I don't want to cum, not right now. Think Alexis Think.

I rush to the middle of the bed, lie on my back with pillows fluffed and whispers, "Let Mama taste that dick."

He crawls to me like a lion devouring an antelope.

I open my mouth for my prize and pierce my lips on the head and seductively welcome the rest to my throat.

He widens my legs as his fingers enter my valley. I feel the sweat coming from our workout.

But I am not done yet…

"Turn ova and suck my nectar Behbee."

Now this is the view I want.

His knees up, sucking my clit
My mouth shaking his balls
Three fingers in my pussy
My tongue gliding upward

My right-hand clenches his dick and massage it fast then slow to the rhythm of his tongue.

I feel precum as I circle the entrance of his forbidden land.

My body is getting weak.

I lick my pointing finger at the moment his manhood hardens and my womanhood softens.

Slide my finger in his ass and jack his dick harder until all I want the walls to know is

CUM….

He groans and gyrates with my tongue

I methodically hula hoop my hips in the direction of his fingers

Open my legs wider

He blows on my clit

I blow in his ass

He tightly grabs my thighs and we release our experience in unison.

I comment catching my breath, “That is how to make love.”

Anything is fair game so Man Up!!!

Chapter 12
(Shafiq)

Awakening with the remnants of her pussy on my tongue is remarkable but it is not enough. The hardness of my dick isn't for her but blood. Usually I can stroke my shit reminiscing of all the bodies I mutilated but tonight isn't working.

Looking at my precious angel in her sleep unable to tame the devil created. I slip out of bed, dress and hop in my car to continue a hunt.

I wasn't always like this but after serving three tours in Afghanistan can brainwash the finest of Rangers. There was much pleasure in beheading insurgents while they pissed on themselves.

I came home with a promise to stop and six months went by after my retirement with no urges. One night I had to get out for a few drinks. I sat at the bar, minding my own business when a brunette with a *Jennifer Lopez* ass joined me for casual conversation. Immediately she ranted about her baby's father; like I gave a fuck. Bitch wouldn't stop talking for shit. I pressed my hands over my ears praying she left me the fuck alone.

Screaming voices dashed through my brain, "Kill, Kill, Kill."

Many attempts to keep them quiet but there was no use so I asked, "Excuse me but have you ever sucked dick in an alley?"

She gave the deer in the highlight look, rolls her tongue and replies, "Not lately."

What the fuck? This was easier than I thought.

Escorted her out of the backdoor, pushed her to the ground and unzipped my pants.

She looked up and smiled, “Big Fella huh?”

Wrapped my hands around her head, force fed my dick while she hummed and sucked.

“Oh shit! I’m going to cum, don’t fucking move.”

Her head game was serious and I never came fast in my life. Maybe it was her throat or the fact I was about to snap this bitch’s neck. She didn’t want to swallow and attempted to break free.

“Naw bitch you drinking.” I spoke in a demented voice.

I squeezed her face with my hand, spun her head around until it snapped back. The limpness of her head fell on my dick. Nothing like busting a nut in a dead bitch’s mouth. Lifted her body, tossed it in the dumpster and headed back to finish my drink.

“Whoa Shit!” Damn I almost ran off the road thinking about that skank. Glad I left *Spearfish* since my killings became an everyday occurrence. Luckily, I was very secretive and left no witnesses.

I arrive on *Tchoupitoulas St* by the *Walmart Supercenter.* I park, roll a shopping cart and count my potential preys.

Bingo!

After picking up some items, I stand in the line behind a young lady arguing with the clerk.

“Look, I gave you a $50 bill.” She says patting her pocket.

“Ma’am, you gave me a $20 and you have a balance of $12.00. Which item are you putting back?”

"Put back, bitch you owe me some change."

I quickly interject with my wallet, "It's okay, add these please."

The clerk rolls her eyes at the customer, looks down and scans the remaining items.

The young lady says, "You don't have to do that. I know what the fuck I gave her." As she puts the bags in the cart and leaves.

"Calm down, it's no big deal."

I gather my groceries and head towards the parking lot.

She puts the cart in front of another car and walks pass me. I peek my head out the window and asks, "Do you need a ride?"

She jumps and answers, "I didn't even see you but no thank you, I stay at the *Centennial Park Apartments* up the street."

"It's too dangerous to be by yourself. Besides you may need a little help with those bags."

"I am sorry but I don't know you to be getting in your car. I will be fine."

"Okay, I offered." Driving out of the parking spot.

Two of her bags bust in my rear-view mirror as she tries to pick them up. I turn the car around and get more bags from the store.

I walk to her and say, "Here you go."

She glances upward and chuckles, "Guess I might need a ride. My name is Sharon."

"and I am Omar."

We laugh and put them in the trunk. I open the passenger side door and take her home.

She says, “I really appreciate this. Not many men would have helped.”

“I am not the typical man besides chivalry isn’t dead.”

Pull up to her apartment, pop the trunk and open the door again.

“Do you need any help inside?”

“Yes, I do if it isn’t too much trouble.”

I can tell she wants to give me the pussy as payment.

Watch….

“No problem, unlock the door and I will bring in the bags.”

She pops her ass cheeks and trots up the stairs.

I pretend not to notice but my dick thickens from the thought.

I bring the groceries inside and grab my keys.

“Take care shorty.”

“Wait a minute. Do you want a drink?”

“It’s late and I wanted to make sure you were safe.”

She touches my hand and begs, “It won’t take long.”

I slowly slide my hand and reply, “Okay but just one.”

I stand in the kitchen visualizing how to kill her. Her voice fades in the distance as I taste the blood in my mind.

As she reaches for the glasses, I stand behind her, kiss her neck and retrieve the knife from the counter. I didn’t wait for her to enjoy it as I slice her slowly.

“Yes indeed, I love the splatter of blood on my face.”

She turns around to say something but I tongue kiss her screams repeatedly jabbing her gut.

I feel the beginning of her last breath and it is turns me the fuck on. I hold her frail body in one hand and jack my dick in the other as her blood and my precum combine.

I throw her on the floor, change knives and stab her again and again and again with excitement. I snatch her clothes off and empty my lust.

I swiftly dress and clean up. Hop in my car satisfied until the hunger starts again.

A dark passenger holds tightly to the steering wheel and says, "You should have gotten some of that pussy. I know it was wet."

"Shafiq, maybe the next one is yours."

Within minutes I am home. Jump in the shower and slide in the bed with my angel.

I clutch her waist and suck her earlobes.

"Eye love u Alexis."

She says softly, "I love you more."

Fear is the best motivated orgasm

Chapter 13
(Alexis)

"Bianca, come to my office when you are free."

"Be right there Boss Lady."

She peeks her head in the door and says, "Is it safe?"

"You good," I reply.

She skips and sits in the chair with her pen and pad asks, "What's up?"

"Call Keith about his availability for lunch today. If he has time, then order po-boys from *Daisy Dukes.*

"Got it. Is there anything else?"

"How many people are here? Also, check on the approval of the Masquerade Party at the pier."

"At the moment, it is five."

"Cool, let me know the RSVP numbers. You got all of that?"

"I got it Boss Lady. I am sorry for the other day." She winks and leaves.

Pick up the desk phone, "Good morning Freddie."

"Hey Tweety, what's going on with you?"

"Not a whole lot. Is everything set for Friday?"

"Yes, it is *Madame*."

"Are you bringing a guest?"

"Hell no, I am collecting my payment."

"No doubt and I have the perfect ThrillPleaser for you. We are pulling out at 8:30 and don't be late."

We continue with a small conversation until Tigri comes in.

"Is everything ok?"

"Do you have a moment?" She asks with hesitation.

"Freddie, I will hit you back in an hour," I say ending the conversation.

Turning my attention to her, "What's going on?"

"I am a little nervous about the party. Do you think I am ready?"

"You have three days to shake it off. Don't stress about anything except having fun."

She takes a few deep breaths, smile and say, "Thank you."

"Set up a date with one of the newbies to take the edge off. Remember, the goal is to develop your clientele."

She gives an understanding nod and leaves.

Staring at my computer and yell, "Fuck!!!!"

Snatch the cell phone out of my purse and dial.

"Hello?" A trembling voice answers.

"Hey, are you okay?" I reply.

"Yeah, I am trying to make it. It is nice to hear from you."

"That's good. I am calling to see if you have any plans for Friday."

"If plans mean *Love and Hip Hop*."

"Oh hell no. I am having a masquerade party. Come out and let your hair down."

"Thank you," her tone changes with excitement, "but I don't have anything to wear."

"Don't worry about it. You are probably a Size 7. I got the perfect dress for you."

"Wow, you are good. What time?"

"Meet me at the pier around 7pm. I will text you the information."

"You have no idea how much I needed this. Thank you so much."

I throw my leg across the arm of the chair and smirk, "Rachael, the pleasure is all mine."

End the call, twirl my hips and say to myself, "Love when a plan comes together."

"Sweeter when it cums harder," a man interrupts my thought.

"You really need to stop creeping up on me."

"The element of surprise is priceless."

"Keith, I am happy you could join me on short notice."

"Anything for you Alex," looking at me up and down then blowing a kiss.

"How do you like being home?"

"It's great. A lot has changed but it is good to see the community rebuilt."

"Yeah but a lot is still to be done. What else is going with you?"

"You!"

"Me, what the hell does that mean?" Giving a dumbfounded look.

"I have a lot to make up for and I want you."

"How the hell you want me when I am not available."

"Alexis, we are soulmates and you know it. Stop fighting and let it be."

Before I tongue lash him, Bianca comes in with the food.

"Boss Lady, here is your *Shrimp and Oyster Po-Boy* and Keith this is your *Roast Beef and Swiss Po-Boy*," she says placing them on the oval table and leaves.

I look at him and point to the chair.

"Alexis?"

"Keith not now."

Bianca returns and says, "*Barq's Red Crème Soda* and water with lemon for you and a *Big Shot Pineapple* for you."

"Serving must be in your blood."

"Damn right, serving vanilla flavored pussy on a platter." Bianca admits and leaves.

I throw the napkin on my lap and divulge, "I am happy with Shafiq and don't want to hear anything crazy again. Enjoy your lunch!"

I immediately get excited as the food touches my mouth; the mixture of mayonnaise and mustard drips to my chin. Side lick and admit, "Ummmmm, this is so good."

"I can imagine how it taste mixed with your pussy."

"Keith, I told you that I didn't want to hear that bullshit."

He jumps up, bends me over, press his forearm in the middle of my back and stick two fingers in my pussy. He slides them out and walks back.

"Are you fucking stupid or something?"

"Not at all. I wanted a taste." He states sucking both fingers to the bottom limb and grins.

"Get the hell out of my office. You have lost your fucking mind."

"Yes and I want you to fix it."

"I don't want to look at your trifling ass. Get out before I call security."

"No problem but I am getting you back even if I have to kill Shafiq. You got that!"

"Are you on drugs or something?"

He guzzles the cold drink, stands and says, “I am not on shit but you heard what I said Alexis. I will see you at the party.”

“Your invitation has been revoked and I am not the same Alexis you think you know so don’t fucking play with me.”

“And neither am I.” He admits slowly out the door.

WHAT THE FUCK JUST HAPPENED!!!!!!

Chapter 14
(Shafiq)

Sitting on the sofa, feet on the coffee table and drinking a cold *Heineken*. Throw on "*Rambo*" by *Bryson Tiller*, look down the street from the window.

I should kick in the door and blow her fucking brains out but Alexis wants to do it differently.

I had arranged for *Two Men and a Truck* to move most of the furniture earlier. The rest can sit to take up a little space until she decides what to do with it.

Tie my laces, ride to *Popeye's* and park in front the house. I am so grateful this neighborhood is quiet and everyone mind their own damn business.

I enter through the back door, up a few steps and see Clarissa sleeping.

I throw the food at her and say, "Today is your lucky day."

She hops up, tries to open the bag with one hand and responds, "Are you letting me go?"

I unlatch her cuffs and answers, "Did you learn anything young lady?"

"Shit I have learned more than I can handle. I want to go home if there is such a thing." She replies choking on her food.

"Take your time. I have arranged for someone to pick you up in a few days."

"Why haven't you killed me?"

I ignore her question, throw a *Red Puma Duffle Bag* and answer, "Here you go."

"I don't know what to say."

"Nothing would be perfect. Finish your food."

I glance at the cleaning supplies in the laundry room and say, "We need to straighten up this pig sty."

"No problem."

She takes a few steps out of the bedroom and cries.

I overlook her tears and suggest, "You can start here and I will start in the other one."

She snatches my face and yell, "I have been in Alexis' house the whole fucking time. I am beating her ass for this shit."

"Take out your frustration on the broom and dust pan. Honestly, your life isn't important threatening my fiancée. Are you begging to get your fucking tongue cut out?"

"Fine, I will keep my comments to myself."

Two hours passed and she hasn't come out of the room.

"Clarissa, you good?"

"This room is full of my clothes, shoes and jewelry."

"Take a quick peek."

She glides to the living room, kitchen, extra bedrooms and bathrooms.

"What the hell is going on? This ain't my fucking house."

"Yes, this has been your home for a year. Alexis didn't think it would be fair to be somewhere unfamiliar. Besides, you were fucking Stephen on the countertops anyway."

"She destroyed my life!"

Throwing her a stack of mail, "No Clarissa, you did that."

"Dirty Motherfucka."

“Yes you are. Instead of being ungrateful, I recommend a hot shower to calm your nerves.”

She looks worse than carcass on the highway. Standing in disbelief for a few minutes, cries and runs in the bathroom.

Take a quick peek at the clock, “Shit, fucking with her dumb ass, I forgot I have things to do.”

Tapping on the bathroom door, “Hey, just a reminder your ride will be here Friday at 8pm.”

“Where am I going?”

“Anywhere you want.”

I turn my head for a second and overhear Clarissa whispering under the running water about how she’s going to report both of us once she is free.

Dumb bitch! Doesn’t she know my ears are super sensitive from my skills as a killer?

I do one last walk through to ensure everything is clean and in the right place. Toss my gloves with the trash and leave out the back door.

Drag the can to the curb and notice an unmarked car in front of the house. The driver and passenger give a nod as we make eye contact.

Thinking to myself as I drive off, “Damn, I wanted to feel her blood on my skin so bad, fuck!”

§§§§§§§§§§§§§§§§§§§§§§§§§§§§§§§§§

(Alexis)

I haven't spoken to Shafiq about the incident with Keith. Honestly, I am unsure how to approach it but something needs to be done.

The ThrillPleasers have instructions to be on the lookout for old and new clients. Everything is in place and I am beyond XXXcited.

I drive to the pier to check on parking arrangements and security. I didn't realize the size of the yacht until planning the masquerade party. All rooms are colored with gray and purple furniture with Harlequin green lighting. The social area and unique atrium allows natural ambience and the kitchen and dining area enhances relaxation. The master room has a king-sized bed with his/her bath space. Exterior lounging area has a wet bar and chaise loungers. The three guest cabins have full size beds and walk in showers.

The chef and bartender will have an array of food and everything from beer, wine, liquor and daiquiris to quench any thirst.

Time for an orgasmic eruption

Chapter 15

I have been running around in circles for the past couple days ensuring perfection. I finally see the hard work paying off with decorations and staff.

The hour is finally here and I am excited watching my entertainers wear cat masquerade masks in various colors symbolizing elegant pussy and dick underneath their garments. They are positioned throughout the boat for pleasure among the waters. This adventure is for the elite and my only goal is providing superb sexual gratification.

A security guard is assigned to a designated area for the finest cocaine and marijuana in case someone needs assistance with their inner freak. Don't worry, the password changes every 30 minutes.

It is 7:15pm and the women show their *Black Girl Magic* in gowns and men sport tuxedos and fitted suits.

I double take as a scent dance across my nostrils. Turn around to follow the masculine attraction. I bite my lip from his feet to the top of his head.

He takes a step towards me and says softly, "Hey Tweety."

"Freddie, my damn cervix opened. What the hell are you wearing?"

"Nothing but a dash of *White Patchouli* by *Tom Ford.* If my cologne does all that, wait until I bless you with my tongue."

He licks the bottom of my cheek to my right ear and nibble on the tip sending tidal waves through my ocean.

"I have the perfect person to assist you with that." I admit taking two steps back.

"If you can't be with the one you love; love the one you are with, right?"

"My point exactly."

We walk into the social area and immediately join the thick crowd.

Shafiq comes from behind and says to me, "Are you ready?"

I jump in his arms and respond, "More than ever."

§§§§§§§§§§§§§§§§§§§§§§§§§§§§§§§§

(Freddie)

It seems I'm the only one on the boat not getting pleased. One of these motherfuckas sharing tonight.

A full moon, beautiful ocean and cool breeze have my dick harder than cement. It is time to spy on some pussy.

Creeping to the first cabin and Latoya stands in crochet boots with identical bra and panties.

Damn! She has this fool crawling on the ground in a matching mask licking his tongue like a happy go lucky puppy AND female thongs.

She yanks the leash and his head flies into her lap. Giving orders to remove her panties, she lifts her legs out one at a time, semi plank over his face and commands to suck her clit.

"Bitch you bit me," she screams.

Pushing his head away with the bottom of her heels, turns and retrieve a leather paddle with diamond stubs.

"Bend over with your no pussy eating ass."

He assumes the position and her first swing is vicious. You would have thought she was beating the mane from a horse. She drops the paddle, walks to the corner and retrieves a dildo.

She rips off the mask and scolds, "Do it right or you will suck the plastic off."

Oh shit! It is the Director of Internal Affairs.

I have seen and heard it all. I'm getting the fuck out of here.

A woman screams two doors down like a banshee. It's amazing how the boat is filled with people and no one cares about the noise.

Fuck that. I'm a nosy motherfucka. I follow her moans like the yellow brick road and discover the wizard or shall I say Adonis.

He lifts her off the bed, carry pass me and instruct her to grab the rails.

"Freddie you want some?"

"Nigga! There won't be any left if you keep fucking her guts out."

He feeds her dick with no sign of mercy. She tilts her head back and screams again.

Adonis fucks the skin off the mayor for thirty minutes. No wonder her face has been glowing lately. I press my fist in my mouth and walk away thinking, "The boat is filled with too many high-ranking professionals. Let me venture to another door."

This one is quiet and captures my attention. Cassandra waves her hand signaling me to come closer. I couldn't see the woman's face since her head is buried in the sheets.

I unzip my pants to relieve the tension of a stressful week. Cassandra wraps her hands around my shaft and massage my worries away while the white woman dangles her feet and continues her meal.

"What about her?" I ask.

"She's paying good money to slurp my juices. I am working on number 4."

Cassandra didn't miss a beat conversing and stroking my dick. Her motions are swift on the verge of climaxing. She squeezes my nut sack and prepares to cum.

A slight exciting expression appears on my face but I refuse to be intimidated. I breathe through my nose and force a smile.

She runs her tongue around her lips and asks, "Can I kiss it."

I shrug my shoulders and reply, "Sure."

My mushroom tip pops in her mouth like a *Super Mario* cartridge; inching closer slowly gravitating me in.

"Damn!"

Her moist tongue wraps around my flesh, "You will cum before me."

She pushes her head deeper into her pussy while deep throating me.

I've been in this room fifteen minutes and haven't seen her face yet. Maybe women eat pussy better after all.

I flip in her mouth and groan to bust. I rock my ass to feed her faster. The female humps the bed while eating Cassandra's pussy.

This is a one beautiful fucking scene.

"Eww Wee."

Grab a fist full of Cassandra's hair, pumps harder and looks in her eyes, "Bitch you getting this nut."

My stomach churns and eyes water, "Oh shit!" I erupt and she swallows every drop. My dick goes limp and oozes from her mouth.

She looks at me and points toward the door, "Get out."

"What the fuck happened? Alexis has these bitches on steroids or something." Laughing from my statement. I zip my pants and do as I am told.

Order a *Long Island Iced Tea* from the bar and walk happily to my last room but sidetrack seeing people snorting powder and rolling Kush.

"Are you enjoying yourself?" A voice asks from the hall.

I turn and answer, "Hell yeah Tweety. You know how to throw a motherfucking party."

She taps my shoulder and says, "Good, let me know if you want a private session with one of them."

Before I answer, she leaves. Alexis has always been the one that got away but never had the nerve to tell her. It seems her new man keeps a twinkle in her eye. Oh well but I will fuck the air out of her lungs.

Creeping into a room filled with cranberry mandarin scented candles while two silhouettes make love to *Burn Slow* by *Ro James*.

I crack the door and sit by the foot of the bed. An older woman rides her man's dick like galloping smoothly through *Audubon Park*.

Hearing the passionate sounds of enjoyment makes me envy their emotions and sexual connection.

Someone runs a fingernail around my neck and startles me for a moment. A woman undresses out of her gown with a red and gold mask.

She pulls her in and says, "I was wondering what gift Alexis had for us."

"Mr. and Mrs. Fountaine, please accept my body to make up for my tardiness."

Thinking to myself, "I cannot believe this shit. The Councilman and his attorney wife are freaks. I got to see how this is going pan out." I sit with my legs open and continue drinking.

The chick darts her tongue through his mouth. He moans softly as his wife continues to ride.

"Rachael please give me permission to be inside of you." He asks.

She looks at Mrs. Fountaine and nods her head, switching positions and granting Rachael the pleasure of mounting her husband.

I take another sip, admire the intoxicating hip rotations and listen to pure sensuality. Tonight, is auditioning time.

She spins backwards and whispers to Mrs. Fountaine, "Kiss my breasts and slide two fingers in your slit."

She greedily obliges and strokes her clitoris. She covers her nipples with her mouth. Both produces love sounds as Mr. Fountaine thrust his love inside of Rachael. I could easily leave but the anticipation of seeing them cum is invaluable.

Rachael pace heightens. Mrs. Fountaine stops and her titties flap against her. Mr. Fountaine spreads her cheeks and pounds from behind. His wife has four fingers inside of her pussy and groans harder.

She pulls them out and Rachael sucks slowly sliding her tongue between her hands.

"Oh Yes!" Mr. Fountaine yells, "Fuck me harder."

She pounces while Mrs. Fountaine fist fucks her pussy. She squeezes her clit, releases and flickers her lips until juices squirt on the sheets.

Rachael screams, "I'm cumming too. Yes, Fuck me!"

This is the moment I've been waiting on. I gulp the rest of my drink, stand up and cheer on their orgasms.

"Mr. Fountaine you better give it all to her."

He thrusts wilder, rocking the bed and calling out her name. Mrs. Fountaine walks over and sticks her tongue in his ear. This must his sensitive spot because he cums instantly.

Rachael twirls her hips again and saturates his dick.

She didn't make a sound during the orgasm. After the ride, she rises and looks in my direction.

She stands in front of me, sticks one finger in her pussy and wipes it under my nose.

"Smell my addiction. This is dope fiend pussy."

She gets dress and I head out the door with another smile on my face.

Tonight couldn't get any better but…….

Grab the vibrating phone from my pocket, "Hello."

Sweet adventure is better while tasting.

Chapter 16
(Anthony)

"Why hasn't this bitch answered my calls?" Stephen ask slamming the phone.

"Calm the fuck down man. I will see if I can reach her." I answer snatching it off the coffee table and dialing Rachael's number.

"I am beating her ass." Stephen yells.

"I gave you the benefit of the doubt when she called me. What the fuck were you thinking? Now you are talking about putting your hands on her?"

"She hasn't responded to my calls or texts. She probably fucking another man." He yells again while kicking the table.

"You claim to still be in love with Alexis but acting like Rachael has a hold on you."

Looking at the clock on the wall, "Do you see what fucking time it is? Do you?"

"Watch your tone nigga, I ain't her. You stepping out of line Patna."

"My bad bruh. She left upset around 6pm and here it is three in the morning. Ain't shit open now but mouth and legs."

"Did ya'll have an argument or something? You need to cut your losses before it is too late."

"Lately, that is all we do; I can't leave her, I love her."

"Don't start talking love with me Stephen."

Before he utters another word, my phone rings, "Hello."

I put it on speaker and a male voice tells me about patrols on the way to the house we used to hang at."

"Who the hell is this?" I ask.

"I am your fucking wakeup call bitch."

The anonymous caller hangs up and for a quick second I am speechless.

"Who was that?" Stephen questions.

"I don't know but…."

He looks at his vibrating phone and asks, "Rachael, where the fuck are you?"

"Swallowing cum," a male voice answers with laughter.

"I don't know what kind of fucking games you playing or how you got my old lady's phone. You got the wrong one playa."

"Nah nigga, I got the right one. My dick was all down your bitch's throat."

"What the fuck did you say?" He asks jumping from the sofa.

"Smell her breath." The male voice responds and disconnects the call.

He looks at me with disgust, "Fuck that!"

I stand, snatch his keys and say, "Let's go for a ride."

"What you mean go for ride? This nigga said he was fucking Rachael."

"Maybe he is but we need to ride to the lakefront."

"Man, we haven't been there since Alexis' fired us."

I go to the kitchen saying, "True but these calls ain't no coincidence."

I grab my black bag from the cabinet and return to the living room. I squat by the coffee table, prepare my shit in four, snort a few lines and say hyper as hell, "Let's go nigga."

"I am ready."

We drive 20 minutes to the fuck house. Turn the corner and two red police cars, crime tape and coroner van are parked.

"I hope that stank bitch Alexis is in there. That type of shit would make my fucking morning better than cheese grits." I yell.

"What the fuck is wrong with you?"

"Man, fuck that hoe. Let's see what is going on."

We get out and scope the area.

"What's going on officer?"

"It's Detective and why are you here?" He snaps.

"We came from the club and saw the lights." Stephen interjects.

"Well stand over there because I don't need ya'll interfering with my investigation."

"Look nigga, who the fuck is in there?" I ask looking over his shoulder.

"A little compassion would be great. Don't know yet still looking for identification. We have everything under control besides if we find any evidence of a robbery you would be the first to know." He sarcastically answers.

We stand contemplating how to find out what happened for a few minutes.

As the Detective stand by the door entrance, he speaks to another officer and points in our direction.

Moments later he returns with his notepad and another Detective saying, “Well, I have a tidbit of information for you.”

“Okay?” I reply aggravated.

“I need you to follow Detective Petit and he will tell you everything and Stephen you can come with me.”

“What the fuck you mean follow him? Nah tell me what the fuck you have to say right here,” I say grabbing my holster.

“Oh, I see we got *Quickdraw McGraw*.” The other Detective says.

“Look, can someone please tell us what is going on?” Stephen pleads.

“We can tell you everything at the station.”

“Being an escort wasn’t how I expected my morning to be. I hope Rachael is okay?” Stephen mumbles.

“Get your fucking hands off me bruh!!” I yell as the Detective pushes my head in the car.

I am your friend to the end?

Chapter 17
(Keith)

The more she tries to run, it makes me want her more. I feel like a predator on the hunt for my prey; horny and hungry.

The beauty of a masquerade party is disguise. I knew if I came they wouldn't let me in so I paid one of my coworkers to go in his place. Luckily, no picture identification was required.

Alexis is extremely busy socializing with her guests as I mix in the crowd. I stand by the bar in a *Phantom in the Opera* mask, black tuxedo and black *Chuck Taylors*.

Every time someone speaks to me, I deepen my voice to ensure I am unnoticed among my continuants.

Her new man follows behind like a lost puppy. I would do anything to be her damn pet. I know he is beating the tissue out of that pussy. FUCK!!

I sit in one of the rooms watching a lot of fucking and drugs and still able to be observant of the hallway.

The more I see, the faster my manhood swells.

Fuck it, I snatch my dick out, massage the head and slowly caress the thick vein on the left side. Up and down on my shaft while twisting my wrists enjoying the tingle in my nut sack.

"Damn, this shit feels good."

Continue moving my hand a little faster not to cum but relishing in my surroundings.

I notice a man across the room watching me. He rubs his crotch through his pants and bulge begins to drip.

His eyes never leave my dick as he pounds the air. I feel my erection diminishing from his stare but another part chimes in and makes it harder than before.

Fuck it, if he likes what he sees then like on my nigga but I am getting this nut. With each turn of my right hand, I lift my shirt, rub upwards and pinch my nipples with the left.

I tap in a few deep breaths and imagine my tongue moving across Alexis' velvet tip; barbaric then soft. It is driving her wild as she lifts her hips on tiptoes and spreads her pussy wider for my pleasure.

Slightly turn my head from my imagination and focus on a muse for an experiment. A black slender woman sits in a recliner with her panties and bra on. Her right hand fights her pussy for escape. Her stomach and pelvic moves like a snake reaching for deep waters.

I wonder, "What type of masquerade party is this?"

She tilts the chair to the wall, lifts her leg and continue with her private party.

My dick stretches to meet her but I spit on the head and continue to massage my thickness. I match her stroke for stroke like we fucking in the wilderness.

She opens her eyes for a moment, smiles at me and continues.

Her lake displays in her panties as she fucks the chair and me. I wouldn't mind getting in that chocolate covered pink pussy. From her movements, my dick is extremely happy.

She becomes Alexis and I am determined to cum….in her fucking face.

I walk from the sofa and stand with my stiff dick waiting.

She puts the chair on all fours, pull her hair back and opens wide. She deep throats on the first mouth trick and never removes her hand between her legs.

I slide them between her legs and clasp our fingers together as we search for unsettled territory.

I slow grind her jaw muscles and hold the back of her head for stability.

I insert my index finger in her swollen canal until my knuckles cracks for her g-spot. She sways her hips clockwise and counterclockwise like a belly dancer by enjoying my thickness in her racy mouth.

I tilt her head upwards, snatch my finger and suck it dry while looking at her. Pushes her head backwards to release my missile and straddles the chair. Luckily it is a rocker as well because it increases the intensity behind our strokes.

She rubs her clit faster and I fuck her mouth deeper. Spit is running down and cum screams to be on her tongue.

She lifts one leg, turn sideways and thrust faster. The chair hits the wall harder as I make her feel my dick in her shoulders.

My nut sack kisses her chin and I feel it emptying.

"Yes baby, get that shit." I reply.

Tears fall from her face as she tries to scream while my semen block her vocal chords.

I slide from her mouth and say, "Thank you."

Her reply is a simple smile.

I put my dick in my pants and stare at the glow upon her face.

"May I?" I ask.

"By all means." She responds.

I kneel by her, rip the top of her panties and lick the seat to get a glimpse of her sweetness.

I suck her clit like the juices from a watermelon iceberg. My tongue licks from the top of her mound to the entrance of her ass.

She holds one arm of the chair and the other on the top of my head as she pushes me back to her yoni.

My tongue slowly finds her entrance as she intensely fucks my face.

"Oh shit, stop, stop." She yells.

I slide a finger in her ass and slurp my oral mixture.

Her legs shake and she hits the top of my head, "Oh my goodness, please stop."

My fleshy tissue speaks a language uncontrollable to her body and she jerks.

I feel a splash, back away from her treasure and saturated by her orgasm.

I have never seen a woman squirt before. The pleasure overcomes her as she bites her finger.

"Fuck, I am so sorry," she yells.

"No need to apologize."

She tries to catch her breath between speaking, "This has only happened once; oh, my fucking goodness that was outstanding."

I respond with a smirk and asks, "Would you mind getting another shirt for me?"

"No problem." She gets up from the chair with nothing but a bra and disappears in the crowd.

I clutch her mutilated soaked panties. Put them in my pocket to sniff later and wait for her in our sex chair.

If you can't be with the one you love, fuck the brakes off someone else.

Chapter 18
(Freddie)

"The job is almost complete." A voice responds.

"What the fuck you mean almost?" I respond walking to the deck.

"Look, everything is taken care of, don't sweat it."

"Tyrone, don't make me fuck you up over this shit man. She wants it done now." I say hanging up.

Order another *Long Island Iced Tea* from the bar, sit in the common area and send a quick text.

"30 minutes."

"Everything under control?" Alexis responds.

"Yes."

"Meet me in the master bedroom."

I sit on the couch, close my eyes and enjoy the sound of balls slapping and lips smacking.

A soft voice interrupts my sexual serenade, "Hello Freddie."

I peek through one eye and answer, "Oh hey, what's up?"

"I didn't introduce myself to you earlier but my name is Rachael."

"Hey." I reply nonchalantly.

"Why are you sitting by yourself? You didn't find anything exciting?"

"Everything is exciting but my mind is on other things."

"Let me help you." She insists unzipping my pants.

"Don't unleash the dragon if you're not going to tame it."

"Not at all."

She rubs her palm between my legs and pulls my dick from my boxers. My legs widen as my pants rests on my ankles.

She flutters her tongue on the head like an audition for *Drumline*. She gulps to the bottom of my shaft and slowly suck to the mushroom tip continuously.

After the third introduction of her skills, it slides further pass her throat and tonsils. She pops her head up and down until I forget people are in the room. I slide one leg out and wrap it around her back. Slouch down, grab her hair and try my best to fuck her eyes out.

She unleashes my dick and says, "Don't hold back; cum for me."

I look down and say, "It's going to take more than this."

She pulls her gown up, sticks her finger in her pussy and says, "I got cotton candy."

"I bet you do but…......"

The phone vibration snaps me back to reality. "Hello."

"Do we need a cleanup crew or what?"

"Naw, none of that shit is required."

"Bet that. Shit is done."

I give a polite grin and say, "It's been real but I got to go."

"Let me finish, please."

"Maybe another time."

Pull up my clothes and head to the master bedroom.

Pass through several rooms with drugs and fucking at full speed.

Skim over my clothes and knock on the bedroom door.

"Come in," A male voice responds.

Alexis lays in the bed dressed in an elegant purple and black laced mermaid gown.

I open my mouth and she interrupts, "Hello Frederick, I would like you to meet my fiancée Shafiq."

"It is a pleasure to finally see the mystery man."

I extend my hand and he responds, "I don't shake hands."

"I understand, no worries."

Alexis interjects, "Is your evening enjoyable?"

"In more ways than one."

I hear the vibration in my pocket again and hurriedly answer my phone.

"Hello."

"It's finished."

"I am putting you on speakerphone. Now give me a run down on what happened?"

Tyrone answers, "She was being a total bitch saying how she wanted to go to the police station. We convinced her to calm down by drinking shots of *Jose Cuervo* and snort a little powder."

"And?" Freddie insists.

"After a few hours, music was played and she wanted to dance. In the middle of "*How does it feel*" by *D'Angelo*, she took off her clothes and started kissing Ricky. Long story short Ricky fucked her then Dominic."

"What the hell were you doing?" Shafiq asked.

"I was making sure shit didn't go too far but after a few rounds shit changed." Tyrone responds.

As he tells the details, Alexis hands are between her legs. The more he speaks, her hips twirl like a baton. She looks at Shafiq, bites her bottom lip and continue with her sexual artistry.

Shafiq clears his throat when he notices the delight on my face. I turn sideways and listen to Tyrone.

"Look ya'll, Derrick came in to make sure she was feeling good. She fell back on the bed and smiled. He picked her up, put some coke on the side of his shaft. She snorted it then sucked his dick while Ricky fucked her in the ass. She was moaning and enjoying everything."

"Oh shit. Is that it?"

"Dominic and I made sure bottles, glasses and plates were put in the trunk. When we came back from getting rid of everything at the *Gentilly Landfill*, she was dead. We did a final walk through, cleaned everything with light bleach, left the evidence and bounced."

I can hear Alexis worries escape her essence. I glance over and Shafiq face is hidden under her gown fighting for her orgasm on his tongue.

"Thank you, Tyrone. We will speak in person on Monday," Alexis speaks through heavy breathing.

"Looking forward to it Boss Lady. Freddie, hit me tomorrow."

We end the call and I stand in awe as I see the beauty in her face.

His hand goes around her neck tasting the explosion of nectar.

I have never imagined her cumming in silence but out of all the events tonight this is the one I enjoy the most.

Shafiq slides from her legs, unleashes her throat and kiss with the kind of passion only seen in the movies.

She finally sits up, licks her lips and says, "Job well done Freddie."

"Damn Tweety, its 4am."

Shafiq responds, "Good timing; you better get you some fun cuz we dock at 6am."

They undress before the end of the sentence. One thing about my ride tonight is not to be self-conscious of seeing another man's dick.

I close the door and continue my adventure.

Voyeurism is beyond a sexy peek.

Chapter 19
(Stephen)

The drive to the police station is intense until I feel like shitting on myself.

What the hell dis nigga got me into?

As we walk pass one of the interrogation rooms, Anthony circles around the chair.

"Bring him to my office," Lieutenant yells from the breakroom.

The Detective escorts me and says, "Have a seat."

He closes the door as I put my head in my hand.

I glance at the clock, jump from my seat when I hear the door opening.

"Your ass is supposed to be handling your personal issues not getting into more trouble Detective."

"Lawrence, I don't have a clue what the hell is going on?" Stephen answers.

"It's Lieutenant!"

"My apologies; what information do you need from me?"

"I don't need anything from you…yet. One of the officers drove your car here so go home. Are we clear?"

"Yes, we are."

He throws my keys and I leave out the back door of the precinct. Sit for a few minutes, stare at 9:00 on the dashboard and cry.

Start the car; drive around to clear my head and board *The Algiers Ferry* to the *Westbank.*

I sit on the railings and admit to myself, “One of many things I miss about Alexis is exploring. I am sure she would love being with me on the water.”

I silently ride across the *Mississippi River* and wonder why my life slowly trickles downhill after being happy for so long.

Finally depart and stop at *General DeGaulle Avenue*. Continue driving and park at *Anytime Fitness* to release some stress and hopefully stop my mixed emotions.

§§§§§§§§§§§§§§§§§§§§§§§§§§§§§§§§

(Anthony)

“Alright Anthony, we have a few questions for you.” The Detective says softly.

“I don’t know nothing bout nothing.” I answer with folded arms.

“Look man. Do you know Clarissa?”

“Yeah, why?”

“Cuz she is dead that’s why.”

I put my hands behind my head and answer, “What the fuck that got to do with me?”

“Nigga it has a lot to do with you.”

“You are out of your rabbit ass mind. I ain’t seen that chick in over a year.”

“Excuse me for a minute.” The Detective announces looking at his phone.

He leaves and the Lieutenant comes in, snatches me by the shirt, pushing against the wall and shouts, “What the fuck is wrong with you Anthony.”

Feeling heated adrenaline rushing through my body, I grab the middle of his shirt, lifts his feet off the ground and throw him on the table.

"Don't you ever put your fucking hands on me?"

The Detective runs in to break us up.

Lieutenant says, "Detective, you are under arrest for assaulting a police officer."

"Bitch you assaulted me. It's on tape dumb fuck." Anthony yells.

The Detective asks while putting my hands in cuffs, "What tape?"

"Beside this bullshit ass charge ya'll trying to get me on; tell me why I am here?"

"Probable cause for now but I am sure within a few days it will change."

"You damn right it will change. I ain't did shit."

§§§§§§§§§§§§§§§§§§§§§§§§§§§§§§§

(Stephen)

Damn, that was a hell of a workout. I should come here more than twice a month.

Swing by *Wendy's* for a quick bite and head to the house.

Take a deep breath and turn the key to open the door. I can sense she is not home. Everything is like I left it…a mess.

Check for missed calls or text messages and nothing. I want to call but unsure since that nigga called me from her phone earlier.

Trying to eat but 12:30 stares me down like *Cujo*. A knock on the door shakes me back to my senses.

I hope it is her and she forgot her keys or something.

Open the door with a smile and quickly it disappears.

"I have a package for Stephen Chambers." A UPS man says with a small envelope.

"I am Stephen." I admit reaching to sign the tablet.

We make an exchange and he says, "Have a wonderful day sir."

I close the door, shake the envelope and place it on the table.

Enjoy the rest of my food as it baffles me on the contents. Snatch it open and a taped note on the DVD falls out.

"I hope you enjoy it as much as I did"

I hurriedly play it and my mouth falls open. Rachael is on her knees, spitting on his tip and deep throating. Bitch never did it for me.

I snatch the flat screen off the wall and scream.

I shake the envelope again and another note falls out.

"Your innocent wife sucks the pulse out of a dick. Thank you!!!"

I destroy every picture of us in the entire house. Rip all her clothes out of the closet and scream again, "Why Rachael, why would you do this to me?"

Houses are easily destroyed with the wrong foundation

Chapter 20
(Alexis)

Peek at a beautiful orange sun over the *Mississippi River* as we get close to docking from our erotic waves.

Shafiq and I admire the sex scent creeping under the doors.

"Hey Behbee, would you mind telling everyone about the final explosion with breakfast in the dining area at 9am?" I ask walking pass a colorful opened door.

"No problem, My Love."

I see Adonis sweating profusely, "Are you okay?"

"I will be when I get some sleep. Damn, I am exhausted."

"How many have you pleased tonight?"

"I stopped at seven but looking forward to their private session." He responds winking.

"Good to hear. Would you mind taking a walk with me?"

"Hell no, my dick needs a nap anyway."

As we roam around, I whisper, "Did you notice everyone mask is off?"

"Someone tapped out!!" Adonis says looking at the Fountaines and Rachael in the middle of the bed.

"Whoever did it first should be penalized?" He responds again waving his tongue like a flag.

"Trust me, this excursion wasn't cheap so tap out if you must but you better get back to sucking her clit or swallowing dick within 30 minutes."

"Damn right cuz time is money."

We glance at each other and bust out laughing down the hallway.

My phone vibrates and stops me in my tracks.

"We got a situation in Room 4." The text displays.

"WTF, on the way."

"Adonis, could you please announce breakfast at 9am? I got to handle something."

"Fuck that, I am going with you just in case."

We make it to the other side and realize I passed it earlier.

Shafiq points then slowly closes the door and says, "Isn't that your ex?"

"What the fuck are you talking about?" I yell.

"Shhhh!"

"Don't fucking shhhh me nigga."

Adonis cracks the door to see who we are talking about.

"Alexis, listen to me closely. Stand your ass out here and shut the hell up."

Shafiq and Adonis quietly goes in and remove everyone except the mystery man and his treat for the evening.

Adonis mumbles to them, "Go to the dining room and we will be there shortly."

I stand in the hallway with arms folded waiting.

A female screams then scuffling and Shafiq hollering, "Nigga what the fuck are you doing on my ship?"

The voice responds, "Fuck you bitch."

Squinting my eyes and thinking out loud, "I know that is not Keith."

Noise gets louder as I enter. Shafiq and Keith are at each other throats. "What the fuck is going on?"

Adonis answers, "I ain't jumping in until I need to."

I say, "LaToya get dressed and bring the girls to the dining room."

She stares at me with hurt in her eyes and walks out.

Keith punches Shafiq in the mouth and blood spurts on me.

Trying to break them apart, "Why are you here?"

Adonis grabs Shafiq, "Look at me! Look at me man!"

I push Keith to the wall and yell, "Answer me."

He licks his lips and answers, "I am not leaving without you."

Adonis blurts, "Damn, this nigga got a death sentence."

Shafiq paces back and forth as the anger festers.

He runs across the room, knocks me across the bed and beats Keith in the corner.

Realizing my soulmate has murder in his pupils and I am unsure if I should stop it.

Adonis yells, "That's enough. Shafiq that's enough before you kill him."

"Get your bitch ass up!" Shafiq commands.

Keith spits blood at his feet and tries to regain his strength. He holds on the wall trying to come to his feet.

"That's all you can do but your mind is fucked up." He says to Shafiq.

He says to me, "Alex, you need to cage your beast before you or he gets killed."

His shirt is blooded, right eye and face swollen. He stands to straighten his clothes.

Adonis jumps in front of Shafiq as he sees the bull excited by the color.

Pointing to Keith, Shafiq sounds through clenched teeth, "We will meet again."

I am astonished about this bullshit transpiring. I stand, take a few breaths and say, “Look, whatever the fuck happened here; stays here. This whole event will not be ruined over this. Do ya’ll motherfuckas understand me? HELLO?” I insist.

Adonis answers, “Got it Boss Lady. I will check on the girls.”

I stare at Keith and he answers, “I am going to sit in here for a while.”

“That’s the best thing you have said this morning. Adonis, have one of the staff bring something to eat.”

“I got you.” He answers shaking his head at Keith and walking out the door.

Shafiq comes over and mutters, “My Love, I am so sorry but…”

I stop him in mid-sentence and responds, “I am done with it, okay?”

“Yes, My Love.”

“Straighten your damn clothes. It ain’t over until everyone is off the boat. Now, let’s eat.”

We walk to the dining room and everyone is laughing, drinking and eating. It is a smorgasbord with grits, omelets, hot sausage links, bacon, pancakes, fried biscuits, and a variety of fruit and wine.

After we sit and relax for a few, I stand, cling the glass and say, “Thank you all for riding on a Creolastic Voyage. Be mindful that your evening has been very discreet. We look forward to bringing more THRILLPLEASURES into your lives soon. Have a wonderful morning.”

Shafiq and I wait at the entrance of the boat with the clipboard to ensure everyone gets off.

"Behbee, I need a serious ass massage."

"You are going to get more than that."

Everyone hugs us as they depart from a successful evening.

The last to come through are Adonis and Keith. He is limping and holding his side.

"Tell Latoya to schedule my private session."

We look at each other shaking our heads then I answer, "I will make sure of it."

Outstanding fellatio gives you brain damage...

Chapter 21
(Stephen)

Pacing from the bedroom to the kitchen, "I can't believe this shit."

I know we have been having issues but to do this is too much for me.

I take a quick peek out of the window as Rachael pulls into the driveway.

I sit on the coffee table and hear scrambling at the keyhole until the door opens.

She walks in with smeared makeup, shoes in hand and staggering with each step.

"Where the fuck have you been?" I ask snapping.

"Why are you yelling?" She answers.

"Yelling, are you fucking serious Rachael. Is that all you can say?" I yell louder.

She drops her shoes, grabs her head and answers, "Shut the fuck up."

She stumbles in the bathroom and closes the door.

I sit in disbelief, contemplating if I should choke her. Instead, I grab her things off the floor and throw them in the bedroom.

Stand by the bathroom door hearing her cry and vomit.

"Rachael, are you okay?" I ask turning the knob.

"Leave me alone."

Thinking to myself, "She is seriously trying my fucking patience."

I open the door and find her sitting on the floor hugging the toilet.

I peek to see a rainbow of shit from her stomach.

"What the fuck did you eat? What the fuck did you drink?" I question her wetting a towel.

I wipe her mouth and try to help her up.

She snatches away and says, "Don't fucking touch me."

She grabs the side of the tub for leverage and stands up.

"Fuck you and this sorry ass marriage." She blurts.

I have had enough; I back hand her and scream, "You are losing your fucking mind. You stay out all night, come home drunk and I got a tape with you sucking the skin off someone's dick. So, fuck you with your trifling ass."

"At least he had something to suck."

I ball my fist and punch her in the stomach.

She bends over and cries.

"Shut the fuck up. Since you want to be a $5 hoe then that's how I will handle you from now on."

I grab her hair and drag her into the bedroom.

"Now suck my dick bitch."

"Get the fuck away from me Stephen. We are done."

"Done? Bitch we ain't done until cum coats your stomach."

She sits on the edge of the bed and unbutton my pants as tears cover her vision.

"You might as well stop with the bullshit. If one tear falls on my dick, I am whipping your ass. NOW SUCK!!!

She lifts my dick out of my pants with disgust.

"Why don't you love me? What did I do?" She asks pathetically.

I snatch my dick away from her, take my pants off and walk to the living room.

I scramble around paperwork and find the disc. My manhood gradually loses it girth as I hold the heartbreaking evidence.

I return to the bedroom and she still sitting in the same position.

I put the disc in and say, "Watch this bullshit!!"

I sit next to her and notice the change in her demeanor and one tear falls to her chin.

"That attention was fucking awesome. If I would have known I was being recorded, I would have done more than that." She says staring in my eyes.

"Are you on something?" I reply.

"Let me make you feel just like I did with them."

"I don't know what has happened in 24 hours but you have lost your motherfucking mind Rachael."

I slide away and look at her up and down with disappointment.

She kneels and gulps my dick in seconds. The more she sucks the more I forget what I was mad about.

I lay back with my hands behind my head and close my eyes.

"Don't move, I will be right back."

I remove my shirt, massage my dick and wait.

"Do you love me?" She asks.

"Of course I do."

"I don't love you anymore Stephen but I will fuck you like I do."

I open my eyes and she crawls to my manhood.

"Rachael, why would you say that?"

She licks the head with circular kisses and slowly slide it in her mouth. I jump as she sensually scrapes her teeth against my shaft.

"Now, we are going to make our own movie while watching this one."

I peek at the flickering light on the camcorder.

My dick thickens with each syllable. She straddles and receives my inches; rotate her hips counterclockwise, gets up and sucks her juices off.

I think as my eyes close, "She ain't never did no shit like this."

She slides down, tongue kiss my balls and spreads my legs wider.

I grab her head and slam my dick in her mouth. She gags and continue her deed.

I twirl a few strands of her hair, put my knees up and rotate my hips. "Oh yes! Suck your dick hoe!"

She tilts her head, looks at me and slide more of my manhood until I feel her heavy breathing through her nostrils.

"Ummmmm." She mumbles.

"You don't love me huh?" I question as I thrust harder down her throat.

She shakes her head no.

"Good."

I yank my dick out of her mouth, throw her on the floor and ram my dick in her ass.

"Since you want to be fucked like a slut then every night that is what you will be."

"Ouch, you are hurting me!" She yells.

"Fuck your pain. Our relationship from now on is my pleasure."

"For real Stephen, you are hurting me. Stop!" She yells louder. I spread her ass cheeks and watch my dick go in and out of her tight rectum.

My dick pulsates as I enter her forbidden cave but I can tell her pussy loves it. With every stroke, her muscles pull me in deeper.

"Oh my goodness." She moans softly.

I grab her neck and whisper in her right ear, "You will always love me and this dick."

I pound in her ass until I feel my load ready to release.

I pull out slowly and say, "Now get this nut."

"Baby, I was about to cum; put it back in please."

"Bitch you crazy, do what you got paid to do."

She turns around, sucks her nastiness and within seconds I scream, "Oooooo fuck...fuck…. fuck!!!!!"

I push her away and fall back on the bed. I thought about vomiting but regain my composure.

I turn to her and say, "Turn that shit off and take your ass in the other room."

"What about mine?" She asks patting her pussy.

"Hoe, I am not sticking my dick in that until you tell me everything."

"No fucking problem. You lucky I gave you some. My toys can do a better job anyway." She says slamming the bedroom door.

I stare at the ceiling and cry.

My heart burns from Love and Lust….

Chapter 22
(Bianca)

Throwing bags in the living room, walk to the bedroom and flop in the chaise lounge.

Slowly take off my shoes, rub my ankles to my vanilla hips and say, "I am worn out."

After a few minutes, unpeel my gown from my sweaty body in the mirror and smile.

"Girl, we have to settle down sooner or later." I say finding a small strand of gray hair.

Fill the jetted tub with hot water and *Tokyo Milk Eiffel Tower Bubble Bath.*

Walk to the kitchen, grab a saucer filled with *Garlic Butter Ritz Crackers* and mix a quick *Johnnie Walker Mango Crush* in a mason jar.

I mention as I blend with the steam, "Can't afford to have a hangover never know when Boss Lady will call."

I hurriedly finish my drink in three gulps and enjoy the scent of my bubble bath as I wash away last night's residue.

I wrap the towel around my damp body, grab a *Victoria Secret Red Sweater Knit Stripe Sleep Shirt* and fall within my mattress.

Snuggle with my oversized pillow and try to doze off but the loud ringtone disturbs my relaxation.

Grab my phone from my purse and see an unknown number. Thinking to myself, "I don't have time for stalkers today."

Place it on the nightstand and gradually go deeper between the sheets.

The phone rings again and again. I answer with a sharp tongue, "HELLO!!"

The operator responds, "You have a collect call from an inmate at the *Orleans Parish Prison*. Would you accept?"

I say, "Yes."

Thinking to myself, "What has Alexis done now?"

"Hey Bianca." A male voice answers.

"Who is this?" I reply confused.

"This is Anthony. I am so sorry to call you like this but I need you."

"You have got to be out of your fucking mind?"

"I have been out of my mind for years without you. I don't have anyone else Bianca. I really need you."

"I am listening."

"I am locked up for assaulting a police officer."

"What the fuck is wrong with you?" I ask.

"It's a bullshit ass charge. I need you to be here for my arraignment Monday at 9am."

"Call yo boy Stephen!"

"I did but no answer."

"I will think about it Anthony."

"I understand. Another thing, don't tell Alexis."

"Don't tell me what to do, remember you need me, right?"

"Yeah, you are right."

"Like I said. I will think about it."

"Thank you, Baby Doll."

I answer with immediate goosebumps, "You are welcome," then hangs up.

I send a quick text message to Alexis about the conversation to ensure I can take off.

She is nowhere near as understanding and forgivable as I am but deep down inside I still love him.

Turn on the TV and watch a few episodes of *Leverage* before getting comfortable for a nap.

The last few minutes is interrupted by a newsflash of a homicide in the lakefront area of the city.

How the hell did Mercedes get there so damn fast?

Ms. Toussaint has a perplex look as she reports about the crime, "Standing in front of the house where an African American female has been brutally raped and murdered in this quiet community. Detectives are speaking with neighbors about any information concerning this horrific crime. The female's name has not been released pending accurate identification and next of kin. If anyone knows anything to solve this murder, please contact Crime Stoppers Hotline at 1-877-903-STOP."

I quickly sit up in the bed and yell, "Oh my goodness, that is Alexis house."

Dial her number and yell as soon as she answers, "Alexis are you okay? What is going on at your house?"

She answers calmly, "Nothing, I am relaxing. What's up?"

"Turn on the news or something. A female has been found dead at your Lakefront House."

"That hasn't been my house in over a year Bianca. Girl get some rest and call me later." She answers and hangs up.

I wonder what is going on. I throw on a pair of leggings and tennis shoes and run out of the house.

I drive 30 minutes in silence. As soon as I make the block, see four police cars, crime tape and news reporters. I park three houses from the scene and notice Mercedes on the side of the house in tears.

"Are you okay?" I ask giving her a hug.

"No, I am not. I saw her." She responds through sobbing.

"You saw who?"

"Bianca, I saw her."

"Who did you see Mercedes?" I ask again shaking her shoulders.

"I can't believe someone would do that to her."

"Fuck, who is it?"

She finally answers with devastation, "Clarissa."

"CLARISSA?"

"I recognized the tattoo on her arm."

"Mercedes, are you sure? We haven't heard from her in over a year?"

"I know what I saw." She yells.

"Calm down. I am a shocked also. Did you call Alexis yet?"

"No, I haven't. I knew it was bad blood between them and didn't know how to tell her."

"Don't worry, I will break it to her. Did they say what happened?"

"Yeah but this is off the record."

"Understood, I won't say anything."

"For what I hear, it was a drug overdose and she was raped after the fact."

"Someone raped her after she died?"

"Yeah that is what I heard.

"That is some sick ass shit."

"Exactly my point."

"Did you tell the police that you knew her?"

"Fuck no. I can't be involved in nonsense. I am up for lead reporter and need my name to be clean."

"Bitch ain't nothing clean about you."

She answers with laughter, "True but I ain't swallowing at work and to them I am *Gandhi*'s daughter."

"You are silly. Look, I am going home but please keep me in the loop."

"I will." She responds with a hug.

I look at the house and reminisce of the dicks passed through the doorsill.

As I walk to my car it hits me, "How in the fuck did she get there?"

Devilish intent comes to reality with proper planning...

Chapter 23
(Alexis)

Another day comes and goes of my happiness as the sun peeks across his face.

I kiss his cheek, sit up in the bed and turn on the television to get a glimpse of last night's entertainment.

It's the same ole thing in the Crescent City; robberies, indecent exposure and drugs but for whatever reason murder is my interest.

Change the channel again and love the way one of the reporters sits behind the desk with a designer jacket and spotless smile. Staring at his face to capture the familiarity and it hits me with laughter…. another client.

He reports about the brutal murder in the lakefront community; I hear the details and feel the intensity building inside of me.

I snatch the covers from my body, jump from the bed and stand in the closet.

"Hey My Love, is everything okay?"

I glance at his skin, dreads, hard dick and answer, "Perfection."

He winks and drifts back to sleep.

Thinking to myself, "Where the fuck is my bag?"

This isn't an ordinary bag however one with special effects.

Whispering and licking my lips, "Aha!" as I find a plain purple medium bag.

"Baby, what are you doing over there? Come back to bed."

I stand by the foot of the bed with the bag on my shoulder and asks, "May I have permission to pay respect and honor it as a sacred organ."

He quickly flips over and answers, "Alexis, what are you up to?"

"May I please?" I ask again sliding the covers off the bed.

"Sure."

"No sounds unless I ask."

"Yes ma'am."

I plop the bag at the edge of the bed and grab a few bottles. Quickly run to the kitchen, put hot water in a bowl and return. Turn on my collaboration of sensual sounds to set the mood and blow a kiss.

As I place a few drops of warm coconut oil in my hands, massaging into his skin and moving upwards to the top of his legs when *Johnny Gill* serenades the room with "*Behind Closed Doors*." Working his muscles and applying a little pressure to release any tension.

I get to the lower part of his pelvic bone and massage with my fingertips with small figure eight motions.

"Hmmm." He slowly moans.

"I want you to fully give yourself to me. Enjoy my hands and surrender."

"Yes." He answers opening his eyes.

"Do you prefer your balls stroked gently or firm?"

"It's yours to do whatever." He answers then closes his eyes.

I slowly massage the perineum paying special attention to his "sacred spot". I slide my fingers from the base of his shaft to his ass alternating with circular motions and gently tugging on his delicate skin.

I allow a few drops of oil to drip from the head down to his testicles and stroke up and down sliding slowly towards his ass again.

His facial expression confirms his enjoyment and of course the thickness of his manhood.

He comes close to an orgasm but it is not my goal right now. I gently squeeze the head and say, "Take deep slow breaths and relax behbee."

I move closer and hold his thickness against my inner thigh, touch the tip against my breast then bring it to the outside of my cheek, put it to my lips following with wet kisses.

I lay beside him feeling the deep and intense energy surrounding the room with our mind, body and soul.

When I woke up from a stimulating nap, I hear water running. I open the door and he says, "Finally."

He drapes my locs to one side and kiss my neck to my shoulder blades.

He lifts me on the sink and demands, "Hold on."

He passionately kisses each breast and licks my areoles with finesse. Reaching for my hand and says, "Don't let the water get cold."

I jump from the sink, open the shower door and smile.

"Shafiq, how much do you love me?"

"My Love, any answer is never enough to describe it."

I wet my palm with my tongue and reach for his love and pull him into the shower.

His erectness waits for my next move or command but I let go and throw my head under the water.

"I would die for you Alexis."

"It is not what I crave."

"Tell me and it is done." He mentions again putting two fingers on the side of my hood, stroking up and down and squeezing my clit between his fingers.

As his touch taps on my deep passage, I try to prolong his penetration but quickly open to receive him.

Gradually turn the water off and allow our bodies to saturate in the mist.

He strokes his fingers like a romantic warrior.

The deeper he goes the more my feet escapes gravity. Pushing slowly on my g-spot but fondles hard then fast stimulating my fire. He anticipates my release as my body moves to the rhythm of his limbs.

The soft bites increase to strong marks between my thighs trying to fight through our foreplay.

He removes his fleshy toy, kiss upward, and sucks my leak from his numbs. "Now what do you crave My Love."

"I would love for us to kill Rachel."

He smiles and responds, "That's my girl."

"Now come and get your pussy!" I mention getting out of the shower.

Wet sheets give a clear mind....

Chapter 24
(Bianca)

Sitting on the bench outside of Courtroom 1 and think, "I shouldn't have told him that I would be here."

Alexis wasn't happy when I gave her all the details but I know she is supportive.

Glance at my watch and time is moving slowly. I grab my phone and walk to the door……

I collide into the back of a young lady as she drops her files.

"I am so sorry. I wasn't watching where I was going." I apologetically mention while gathering scattered papers.

She asks in a soft tone, "Bianca?"

I smile and answer, "Funny bumping into you."

"Likewise." she responds.

"Let me help you; it's the least I can do."

"Thanks! How have you been?"

"Wonderful! Life is truly beautiful."

"What are you doing here? If you had a ticket or something I could have taken care of it?"

"No, Chanae it is nothing like that. I am here giving morale support to a friend at his arraignment."

She lifts her eyebrow, puts the remaining papers in the file and says, "These cases are always flipping back and forth. The judge doesn't play and I love how he punishes the guilty which makes my job satisfied. I hope it works out for your friend."

Chanae hasn't changed a bit. Always trying to prove to the world that she can do everything better than a man. I believe she love punishing them because of all her failed relationships. She is overly dominant; probably an undercover butch if you ask me.

"Well don't stand there Bianca. Let's catch the bad guys." She admits dragging my arm.

"You know court rooms makes me nervous. I'm going to rinse my face in the restroom and meet you inside."

"Sure thing!"

Bolting through the bathroom doors, extend my hands to the automatic rinse and dab my face. My makeup is too beautiful to fuck up before seeing Anthony.

§§§§§§§§§§§§§§§§§§§§§§§§§§§§§§§§§

(Anthony)

"This is the final day of a crazy ass weekend and I can't wait for it to be over."

Scanning the courtroom for Stephen or Bianca and divulges, "Where the fuck is my support system, you can't count on anyone these days?"

My moment of pity is interrupted after glancing at the petite female in a stylish blue business suit. She walks up, whispers something to the police officer and mean mugs me.

"Why the fuck is this bitch staring in my face." I mumble under my breath.

She struts away and sits in the back of the courtroom. Opens her briefcase, pulls out a file and gives a devilish smile over her glasses.

"I don't know what the hell her problem is but I swear she is going to fuck around and get smacked when my hands are free."

One of the most impolite things is to stare and don't speak. Deep breaths and clinching my fist, I mumble again, "Let me calm the fuck down before I snap on this hoe."

The officer turns to me and says, "You seem a little tense, no worries we have a relaxing jail cell waiting on your bitch ass. They even give excellent massages. How do you feel about those accommodations?"

I buck my eyes and gradually squint trying to pierce his soul. "You wouldn't talk to me if we were in the precinct Rookie."

I don't know why motherfuckas want to grind my gears but the intensity is setting my mind in motion.

Officer turns around again, force me to my seat and utters, "I will be so happy when your bitch ass goes down in flames."

"Listen Rook, once these charges are dropped, your ass belongs to me. Heed my warning; do your job, shut up, and go home to your little family. I know more people than you think."

He paused for a second, shifted his weight on his left foot and stood in silence.

"Bout damn time," I thought. His breath was stinking any damn way.

Chapter 25
(Anthony)

The Court Reporter shouts, “Case # 161101.”

I am escorted to the front of the courtroom with a *Chester the Cheetah* grin when my eyes sweep across Bianca’s face. She is sexy as always and once I post bail, I’m putting my dick in all her holes.

The judge eyeballs me with despondency as he sweeps through the file.

He clears his throat and says, “Mr. Anthony Benjamin, you are hereby charged with attempted manslaughter and aggravated assault on a police officer.”

“Are you fucking serious?” I interject.

“Mr. Benjamin, I advise you to be quiet or be held in contempt. Are we clear?”

“Yes Sir.”

“You have been advised of your constitutional rights. If you are not able to hire an attorney, then the court will appoint one for you. How do your plea?”

“No contest Your Honor. I don’t need a public defender; save his ass for the low baller street thugs behind me.”

The courtroom erupts in laughter.

“Order in the court!” The judge demands while pounding the gavel.

“Mr. Benjamin, you have one more time to interrupt my courtroom and I will make sure you serve your time until your hearing. Do you understand?”

"Yes Sir!"

"Ms. Carmichael does the state have a reason to deny bail."

"Your Honor the defendant is a menace to society with a badge. He has a history of harassing local street dealers, sleeping with escorts and we have witness statements about keeping evidence from robberies. The list grows with every case he is assigned. I understand he has been a police officer for a long time but he is evil. May I approach the bench?"

She walks up, hands the judge some papers and he thoroughly scans them.

Who the fuck is she? I will have her family heads for a Saturday cookout.

After reviewing the documents, he hands them back and winks in my direction. I already know what time it is and so will she.

"Mr. Benjamin, you are an upstanding citizen of this community and the *New Orleans Police Department*. I hereby release you on your own recognizance. You will return to court on December 29, 2016. If you fail to appear a bench warrant will be issued and your chances of having a reasonable bail will be eliminated. Will you comply?"

"Yes, Your Honor, I will."

"Make sure to contact your attorney. You are free to go."

The judge looks at the court reporter and she announces, "Case # 161116."

"Free to go! Your Honor there must be a mistake." Ms Carmichael interrupts.

"Your documents are not sufficed. Please bring a witness, video tape, or deeper evidence to justify Mr. Benjamin was in the wrong at the trial."

She huffs, slams her paperwork inside the brief case and storms out the courtroom.

Brushing against the rookie cop I state, "Son you have witnessed an iconic officer. You heard the judge mention I am upstanding."

He didn't respond. I run pass him, kiss Bianca fine ass, and tell her to meet me outside. I taste her tongue for a split second before being snatched by the bailiff.

That is what you call a victory kiss in my world. Before I could raise my hands, Ms. Carmichael comes through the door.

"Your Honor this is a prime example why we are dealing with a primate with a badge."

She points toward me and says, "Mr. Benjamin this case is far from over."

"I am sure there is an explanation for this misunderstanding. Anthony will never hurt anyone." Bianca stands and blurts.

Ms. Carmichael throws her hands up in awe. "He is the friend huh? You are defending this fruitcake."

Bianca puts her head down and answers, "Yes."

"Baby you don't have to ashamed of me." I yell being escorted through the cage

"Bianca, you can be with anyone. Why would you waste your time on him?"

I scream, "I love you," shaking the courtroom.

"Snap out of it woman. You act like he is *Michael Ealy*."

"Be quiet Chanae. I still have love for him."

"Please protect yourself. I don't trust him as far as I can throw a car."

"Give him a chance."

"Chance? Are you delusional Bianca? He is charged with attempted manslaughter and aggravated assault and who knows what else. I'll give him a chance to rot in hell. Don't be stupid Bianca."

"I am going to be there because he needs me."

"Okay, but when I convict his ass, don't have a lemon face."

"Convict him?"

"If you wouldn't have been drooling over him. You would have seen me down there trying to keep him from posting bail. I am the prosecutor for his case and plan on making sure he gets as much time as possible."

"Chanae, please don't do this, please?" She begs and cries.

"Stand by your man and go down with him. Alexis gave you too much credit because what I see is a dumb white bitch that will sell her soul for black dick."

"Fuck you Chanae! You didn't have to go there."

A gigantic smile comes across my face as I witness my baby cussing her ass out. Ms. Carmichael walks out the courtroom and I want to kiss her again.

The Bailiff hurriedly snatches me in mid-stride and escort me for out-processing.

Stupidity is the new Reality for Loneliness….

Chapter 26
(Rachael)

The best way to get over a man is to fuck another one. Ever since I realized what makes me happy, I give less than a damn about Stephen's feelings or our marriage.

Grab a *Forever 21 Black Off the Shoulder Jumpsuit* with *Strappy Lace-Up Stilettos* out of the closet and make a call.

"I would love to see you today? Are you available?" I ask the male on the other end.

"I am for you. What do you have planned?" He answers.

"Something a little different."

"Sub?"

"Sure." I answer without hesitation. "Meet me at Majestic Pleasures in two hours."

As soon as the call disconnects a hot flash comes across my body. I run to the bathroom and vomit from the door to the toilet.

Oh shit! What the hell have I agreed to. Just imagining it makes me nervous, exciting and fearful.

Brush my teeth, run my finger to straighten my hair and make another call.

"Is Alexis in her office?" I ask.

"May I ask your name?" Female answers.

"Girl, I am so sorry, this is Rachael."

She lets out a sigh, "Yeah she is in there, let me transfer you."

"Hey Boss Lady, Rachael's crazy ass is on the line. You want to speak to her or send to your voicemail?" She asks.

"Rachael huh? No LaToya send her through. I am pretty sure it will be worthwhile."

After a brief pause, Alexis says, "Well hello stranger, what's going on?"

"Nothing much. I have a client and checking to see if the Thriller Room is available."

Alexis responds with shock, "You have got to be kidding me; the Thriller Room?"

"Don't laugh Alex it is my client's request and I want to make him happy."

"Okay, what time?"

"He should be there within two hours and I am on my way."

"Good because you need to see the space before you are engaged. Can I ask you a question?"

"Of course."

"Who is the slave?"

"Slave? Ain't nobody said shit about a slave." Rachael yells.

"Poor baby, you have no idea."

As soon as I hang up the phone and step out of the bathroom, Stephen stands in the doorway and asks, "Where the fuck are you going dressed like a high-priced whore?"

I quickly brush pass and say on the way to my room, "Wherever is my fucking business."

I throw some clothes in a bag, snatch his keys off the kitchen island and say, "I'm out Bitch."

Halfway to the bookstore, I stop at *Sidney's Saloon.* Nothing is more deserving than a drink or two to settle my nerves.

Find a seat at the bar and order two glasses of vodka and orange juice with a shot of *Jägermeister*. The first one disappear rapidly leaving a nice warm inner glow.

I sip the second one slowly and feel the relaxation taking over my body in ways never felt before.

I stand up from the bar, feeling a little tipsy but ready to face my adventure with Keith.

Twenty minutes across the bridge, park on the side and take a few deep and intense breaths.

Walking through the door and Alexis stands with a notepad and a sly grin.

"About damn time. What took you so long?" She asks.

"I..."

"Oh hell no, your ass been drinking? That is not how a ThrillPleaser carry herself." She quickly interrupts.

"I am so sorry Boss Lady. Let me get my bag out of the car."

I damn near stumble over the curb sprinting to the car. Unzip the side pocket, take a fingernail full, sniff and calmly return.

"Tyrone, can you please make her ass an *Iced Caramel Macchiato with triple expresso* and bring to the Thriller Room?"

"No problem Ms. Roulle."

She throws the notepad to my chest and says, "You better take quick notes."

We pass a few doors, turn right and stand in the hallway. She mentions, “If you are uncomfortable, say the safe word.”

“Safe word?” I question with confusion.

“Yeah muthafucka, safe word. If he wants you to do something, he will not ask, he will tell you. On the other hand, if you want something done, you will not ask instead you will beg. Understood?”

She opens the door to a dark room with a black and gold sign on the wall displaying,

“SACRED SECRETS”

Tyrone comes down the hall, stops in front of Alexis and passes the drink to me.

“Ms. Roulle, there is a gentleman in the lobby. Do you want me to bring him back here?” He asks.

“Oh, my goodness, I am going to be sick.”

I gulp the large coffee and run to the bathroom inside the room.

“Tell him that I will be there in a minute. You can go for the night. I will see you at noon tomorrow.”

“Are you sure because I can stay if you need me?” He insists.

“You may have a point.”

He leaves and Alexis closes the door behind us.

I peek out of the bathroom and says, “I can’t do this.”

“I don’t have time to explain everything in the room but be very obedient and have fun.”

"Alex, did you hear me.?"

"Nipple clamps, floggers, blindfolds, hoods and spanking paddles are to your left.

"ALEX?"

"Bondage harness, cuffs, ropes and collar are to your right. Behind you is the bondage bed and bench with corset and gag ball. Next time, be careful of the unknown. I advise you to absorb your surrounding while I get your client."

"Time to play my way!!!!"

Chapter 27
(Alexis)

"Well. Well...well." I announce down the hallway.

"Hello Alexis, looking good as always." He answers with a smile.

"This is your first time as a client of Majestic Pleasures and we need to discuss a few rules. Do not leave any marks on the arms, legs or above the neck. Also, make sure she knows plum is the safe word."

"Hmmm, you are sexy as fuck in business mode."

"This is about money and enjoyment. I need to put your credit card information on file. Are you aware of the fee for this service?"

He steps closer, waves his tongue and answers, "I am aware of everything."

"Keith, you are not here for me save the roleplaying."

He hands his card and watches me to my desk.

Tyrone yells across the lobby, "Hey Boss Lady, do you want the usual?"

"Nah, but you can give me two shots of *Grand Marnier* and a *Heineken* for our client."

I scan the card, print the receipt and hand it to Keith, "Follow me."

"Damn I want you Alex." He whispers.

"A few days ago, you wanted LaToya but you paying for Rachael. Irony huh?"

"I can imagine my dick beating on your clit. Wait a minute, who the hell is Rachael?"

"Damn, you made an appointment with her. Don't worry, I won't tell LaToya."

We stand on the outside of the door and I mention, "Being in my life demands an extreme level of loyalty Keith. You aren't ready for such as task."

"I am more than ready."

"We shall see." I open the door and Rachael stands awkward and restless.

He turns to her saying, "Good evening my dear."

I close the door with calculating thoughts and hum to my office.

§§§§§§§§§§§§§§§§§§§§§§§§§§§§§§§§§

(Keith)

I take a fraction of a second to change my facial expression into a submission trance.

Walk to the bar I say, "Find something to wear."

Her voice trembles, "You don't like what I have on?"

"I haven't touched you and the wetness soaks your jumpsuit crotch. Grab four items and change. Please don't make me do it for you." I unapologetically answers pouring a drink.

She walks around the room, picks up nipple clamps, corset with gag ball and spanking paddle.

She slowly removes her clothes and asks, "Is this good enough?"

"No questions."

She stands shaking while sliding her flesh into the corset. I can tell she is scared not for what I will do but whether she will enjoy it.

I jump on the bed and command, "Come here!"

I snatch her titties from the corset upon her arrival. Dipping my finger in the *Honey Jack Daniels,* circle her nipple and watch her eyes clench shut, "Look at me!!"

Her eyes quickly snap back as I suck the tip of her areola. "Keep your eyes open; you will call me Master as I prepare to fuck you."

"Is it going to hurt?"

"Yes, it is going to hurt so much you'll squirt in my hand."

I continue sucking her breast shamelessly, filling her with erotic sensation sending streaks of pleasure to her pussy.

I shift lower and pull her legs up and apart, spreading her pussy and plucking my finger against her clit. She gasps and exuberance vanishes as my grip on her legs becomes increasingly rough.

I lift them so high until her knees crush her breasts. I can tell she has never had this type of exposure and arousal.

Continue massaging her clit with the tip. Her pussy spasms in minutes with euphoric orgasm beneath my skillful finger.

She returns from a blissful haze by opening her eyes. Her breath stops when I give a bewildered stare as if she betrayed me and say, "We are done for now."

She quickly sits up and asks, "Did I do something wrong?"

"What did I tell you about asking questions Rachael?"

I reach for the spanking paddle and ask the question again.

"I am so sorry, please don't hit me."

"I won't hit you. I will spank you like the disobedient bitch you are."

She puts her finger in her mouth, twirl the ends of her hair and says, "Spank me Master."

I don't know if I want to bite her lips or see them wrap around my dick from her comment.

She leans over my lap, unzips my pants and takes my dick out.

"I didn't tell you to touch me." I say spanking her left cheek.

She jumps and her pussy gets wetter.

I take a handful of hair and spank her again seeing her treasure throbbing spasmodically.

"Yes." She moans softly.

"I see you like that. Stand by the bed."

I grab the nipple clamps, rope and meet her within seconds.

"This will be uncomfortable for a while but if the pain is too much the safe word is plum." I state tying her hands behind her back.

I guide her to a kneeling position on the floor and lift my dick to her face. I want to see her eyes of innocence as I pump my dick her mouth.

I gradually put the head on her lips and instruct, "Open."

She quickly obeys with the rushing of a tunnel greeting the morning traffic.

As my shaft feels her tongue, I slide a clamp to her left nipple. She jumps and continues with intrigued eyes.

"Do you want to make me cum?"

She nods with a childlike appearance.

"I am happy to know that. Now suck your dick little girl." I mumble doing the same to the right nipple.

The deeper she sucks the tighter the clamps become until minutes later she is only concerned with pleasing me.

I raise my feet and massage her clit with my toes. Feeling her flood pulsates my dick attentively down her throat.

By the look on her face, her enjoyment is better than mine and it angers me.

I snatch the left clamp off and push her down. As my dick leaves her mouth she coughs and sheds a tear.

"What is wrong Master?"

I slap her face with a threatening tone, "What the fuck did I tell you earlier about the questions bitch?"

A harder slap happens when the door busts open.

"Do we need to discuss the rules again?" Tyrone suggests.

§§§§§§§§§§§§§§§§§§§§§§§§§§§§§§§§

(Alexis)

"Damn, someone has an aggressive nature since we last met." I admit looking at the computer screens.

I shift my position in the chair to seize the throbbing ache between my legs.

He face fucks Rachael with no regards of her poor gag reflex.

The more his dick rotates in her mouth my eyes match his strokes.

“Fuck this, I want to see this in person?”

I rush out of my office and head to the Thriller Room. As I turn down the hallway, I run into Tyrone leaving the room.

“What are you doing down here?” I ask with laughter.

“Boss Lady, I am always walking around and checking on the store before I leave. I heard a noise and barged in to remind your client about the rules.”

“Is that right?”

“Yes, it is…He was about to taste some of these shells before I heard your steps.” He admits patting his side.

“That is good to know Tyrone. Thank you very much. I will take it from here but I need for you to be on the lookout for Shafiq.”

“No problem.” He answers walking towards the lobby.

I bust through the door and Rachael’s hands are tied to the bed, wearing a corset and legs spread in a “V”.

Her brown and pink fountain slowly pours on the mat.

I sit in the corner and continue my obsession.

“Would you like to join us?” Keith asks.

“I will in a few.” I answer sliding out of my pants showing my crotch less panties.

I make a gesture for Keith to sit between my legs as Rachael watches.

“Lick my pussy like the dog you are?”

“Yes Mistress.”

He slowly laps around my mound, down my clit and enters my pussy with his tongue.

"Did I tell you to do that?" I ask with a smack across his head.

"Where you fucked up Rachael is letting him be in control?" I announce snatching his shirt and dragging him to the bed.

I point to the direction of where I want him to stand then throw my leg over her face and say, "I am always pulling the strings."

"Now, you will fuck her until I cum. If you cum before me, I am going to kill her." I demand getting my purple and black leather gloves.

"Wait a minute; you see my dick. I can't make that kind of promise." He announces stroking his manhood.

Rachael scrambles to break free from the bed post screaming, "Alexis, please let me go."

I respond, "You wanted to play with the big kids so it is time for initiation," as I slip on my gloves and squat over her face.

Keith blows a kiss and rams his dick into her until she bounces at my entrance.

The more she squirms the deeper his thrust becomes and I feel the intensity begging for an introduction.

I perform geometric equations on her nose until her tongue taste my sweetness little by little.

"Hmmmmmm." Keith squeals.

I shake my head, spread my lips and expose my deep pink. She enjoys my treasure; I stick my index and middle fingers inside, twirl it and suck it pass the knuckle.

His eyes allude sexual gratification as he pounds her cervix in the mattress.

He calls out, "Sorry Rachael, I can't hold on any longer."

The harder he hits her spot the faster her tongue plays on my clit.

He rams another stroke and yells, "FUCK!!!"

I snatch the knife from my bra and stab her in the chest. The deeper I cut the wetter my pussy get as I watch the tearing of her skin with each inch. I release the knife from her bosom and lick the blood and smile.

I immediately grab the gag ball as I remove from her face saying, "Do you remember Lulu?"

Her tears flow faster than *Lake Ponchatrain* when Keith unties her left hand from the bed and says with sadness, "We could have done so much."

"This ain't the fucking *OWN* channel. Kill dat Bitch!!"

"I didn't cum yet Tweety."

"Muthafucka neither did I, what is your point. Kill her or I will kill you. Make a fucking choice!!!"

He flips her over as she holds her chest looking at the blood escaping her fingers.

"Lulu was my fucking friend but you sent her a Dear Jane letter in prison. You may not remember her since you were sucking Stephen's dick. She killed herself over your stank ass."

She speaks with gurgle words, "You knew Lulu. Don't do this Alexis. I thought you were my friends."

Keith pumps his dick from the side as I place the gag ball around her mouth.

She tries to fight but I turn her face and say with a kiss on her cheek, "Be very fucking careful of who you call friend."

He lifts her legs and ensure a frisky doggy style position. I put my hand in the middle of her shoulder blades as he pounds harder and fierce.

He immediately puts his hands around her neck as the heat boils between his legs.

She loses consciousness with each destructive thrust. A tear falls from her eyes as her head slightly falls to the side.

Keith screams through his explosion, "What the fuck have I done?"

"You nutted on her back, duh."

I get up and see her lifeless body on the bed and immediately squirt.

"Alex what the fuck is wrong with you?"

"Nothing but sexual adrenaline. I will get Tyrone to help clean up your mess."

"What the fuck you mean my mess; this is our shit."

'Nigga really, I am the only one with gloves."

"Bitch you set me up!!" He screams.

"Nah baby, you had something to prove, remember? Now, you will do what the fuck I say when I say it. You won't be able to piss unless you ask permission. The next time you want to play, think about it…you did this to your mutherfucking self."

I strut to meet Tyrone and say, "Get rid of the body and if he gets smart; get rid of his ass too."

Loyalty is unconditional

Chapter 28
(Anthony)

"What the fuck? I haven't heard from your ass in days." I snap answering the cell.

"Man, the usual marital shit that's all. Enough about me, I am glad you are out."

"I wasn't worried about them bullshit ass charges anyway."

"Bullshit charges?" Stephen questions. "You are crazier than I thought. Bruh, the state has two new cases on you. Malicious wounding on a fellow police officer and murder."

"Murder?"

"Yeah nigga. Didn't you talk to your attorney?"

"Fuck no. My attention has been on Bianca."

"You have got to be kidding? Your attorney has been around the precinct trying to get character witnesses and no one volunteered but me. Wait a minute, did you say Bianca?"

"Ole bitch niggas." I reply throwing a glass against the wall.

Bianca runs in the living room with a concern tone, "Baby, is everything okay?"

"Yeah, I am good. Do you want to go out tonight?"

"That would be nice." She responds with blush cheeks.

"Pick a restaurant and put on something extra sexy. How does that sound?"

"Wonderful. See you around 8pm?"

"Yes baby, see you then."

She gives a big hug and disappears as quickly as she entered.

"Man, sorry about that."

"What the hell are you up to Anthony?"

"Why I have to be up to something?"

"Whatever it is, I don't want to be caught in it."

"Shut your ass up. She was the only one at my bond hearing and stood by my side since the rest of my boys acting like ducks."

"You want to shoot some pool later. Apparently, you have time to waste."

"Gotta do a raincheck on that one. Getting my dick sucked is more important and I have a few things to put in the works."

"Boy, you are a dumb ass." Stephen responds with laughter.

"I have my moments." I admit. "Holla at cha boy later."

"Later." He confirms and hangs up.

I clean up the broken glass, snort my last three lines and log on the computer.

Thinking to myself, "I need the ultimate *Panty Dropper.*"

§§§§§§§§§§§§§§§§§§§§§§§§§§§§§§§§§§

(*Bianca*)

As I take the scenic route home, "*I Do Love You*" by *Avery Sunshine* comes across the radio. I immediately stop in the flow of traffic on *St. Bernard Avenue* and cry.

"Get it together Bianca."

Cars honk around me with signs of aggravated appreciation.

I continue driving and contemplate calling Alexis with the good news since we haven't spoken in a while.

My phone rings with the ThrillPleaser tone and "*Picture This*" by *Adina Howard* displays a smile.

"Hey Bianca, this is LaToya."

"Hey chick, what's up?"

"What's up? I am checking on you."

"Girl I am better than ever. Did Boss Lady tell you to call?"

"Fuck no. I am calling because I haven't seen or heard from you."

"Aww, that is so sweet of you but I am wonderful. How is the store?"

"Busy as fuck. I didn't realize how much stuff you did around here."

"Trained by the best of course." I respond chuckling.

A few minutes later a controlling tone intervenes, "Make your way here now or you are done."

Before I can respond LaToya says, "She has been on a tyrant attack for days."

"Fuck! I am on my way." I answer with a loud sigh.

"Perfect answer." She says disconnecting the call.

Twenty minutes down the road and I park on the side of the bookstore.

As soon as I make my way to the front desk, LaToya greets with an applause.

"Damn girl, did you bring *New Orleans Finest*?" She asks running to the window.

"You got jokes, I see."

We share a few laughs then I am snatched by the arm.

"What the fuck?" I ask.

"No one has heard from your ass in days so answer your own question Bianca. What the fuck?"

As we walk to her office I respond, "I thought Chanae would have told you that she saw me?"

"No, but Mercedes did." Alexis answered slamming the door.

"She told you who it was at the lakefront house?"

"Yeah she mentioned it."

"Damn Alex, you don't have to be so fucking cold. Clarissa was your best friend since college and you are acting like you didn't know her."

"Fuck Clarissa's dead ass. She deserves whatever the fuck she got. I hope she died with a dick in her throat."

"I knew you were scandalous but to stoop this low is ridiculous."

"You will never know everything about me Bianca and highly recommend not to get caught in my web."

"Is that a threat?"

"I am beyond the threat game. I am only trying to give you what you want; be careful of what you ask of me."

My attention strays from our conversation as the phone vibrates in my purse, "Can't wait to see you later, Love you."

"I got to go." I interrupt her rambling and leaves.

He Loves me He Loves me NOT....

STUDIO20THREE

Chapter 29
(Keith)

"I can't believe Alexis doing this shit to me?" I announce loudly.

Turning to Tyrone but his attention is on his phone.

"Did you hear me?" I ask hitting his arm.

He turns in my direction and answers, "What?"

"Did you hear anything I said?"

"Fuck no! I ain't here to play jeopardy with your ass."

"I was only trying to have small talk. Damn, she has ya'll asses trained?"

"You want your face blown off with dat dumb shit."

As I see the sign to *St. Martinsville*, I ask, "Why did we come out here?"

"This is the place Boss Lady picked; I am only here to do my job. Any questions, hit her up. Follow that road to the park." He answers pointing to the left.

"The park?'

I drive an additional 10 miles before the entrance of *Lake Fausee Pointe State Park.*

An attendant greets us at the gate as the sun disappears behind the trees, "We are closing."

I feel myself panicking when Tyrone says, "We have an appointment."

I put the car in park as he gets out of the car.

A few minutes later, they exchange daps and the gate opens as he backs in.

"What the hell was that about?" I ask.

"Mind your business and drive."

"Drive where?"

"Damn dude, really? Drive until I tell you to stop."

It seems like hours until he says, "Hey, pull over here."

I quickly swerve, park on a rocky trail and open the door.

"What the hell are you doing?" Tyrone yells.

"Getting a dead body out of my damn car."

"Ain't nobody said shit about getting out. Pop the trunk."

I close the door and do as instructed, "What the fuck is going on?"

"Dude, just chill until we get the signal."

"Signal? Who the fuck is out here?"

"As anyone ever said you have bitch tendencies?"

"I ain't no bitch."

"I didn't say you were but you act like one." He answers with laughter. "Follow my lead and you will be fine."

"I want this nightmare to be over."

A few more minutes later, he blurts, "There's the signal."

I jump as the car shakes and hear a loud thump. Two taps on the side of the car, Tyrone opens the door and says, "Let's go!"

I walk behind him as Rachael lifeless body is rolled in a wheelbarrow ahead of us.

"Who is that?" I ask.

"Shhhh."

"Don't shhh me nigga. Who the fuck is that?" I demand.

Our guide stops in midstride and answers, “It will be hard to speak without a tongue.”

Tyrone shakes his head and whispers, “Bitch tendencies.”

We pass a dozen trees, make a hard left and sees a large tarp with supplies.

“Grab a shovel, bag of cement and couple of artificial grass mats.” He instructs.

I give a bewildered look with a loud sigh.

A voice speaks from behind the trees and says, “Bout damn time. Ya’ll niggas out here sightseeing and shit. I am trying to be home before midnight.

The guy followed earlier takes off his shirt and turns in my direction. “Damn, I know him.” I say to myself.

He tilts her body in a hole and says, “Let’s do this.”

Tyrone rushes over, easily empties the wheelbarrow in the makeshift grave and laughs.

Moments later, I realize who it is and yell, “Adonis?”

“What’s up?” He answers without concern.

“Man, she got you too?”

“Who?” He asks.

“That bitch Alexis.”

Seconds later, something hard hits me and I fall to the ground.

§§§§§§§§§§§§§§§§§§§§§§§§§§§§§§§§§§

(Shafiq)

"Thanks for coming out but I didn't need any help." I mention spitting ranch sunflower seeds.

"I am off tomorrow. About time, they are coming through the gate."

"Good., what's going on with you?"

"The usual injured or deceased. Luckily for me, I am having a little bit of fun."

"I hear ya."

"When is the wedding?"

"Adonis, she claims to set a date when the smoke clears."

"Let me meet them." He announces sending four flicks of light.

As we walk through the trees, I drag an ole school tent with supplies and plop it in front of a trunk.

I untie the knot and look at the machete, shovels, bags of cement, turf grass and giggle.

The vibrating sound ceases my humor. "I miss you," displays across my home screen.

I swear she makes me love her more with little gestures. I retrieve the machete and slide it in the rear of my pants.

I take a few steps and think out loud with laughter, "I need some entertainment before I get home."

Rushing to hide behind a tall oak tree as the voices come near.

I snicker as I hear Tyrone saying, "Bitch tendencies."

Adonis points in the direction for them to grab the supplies and my dick gets stiff looking at her brown skin draped over the wheelbarrow.

I readjust myself, come from the shadows, clear my throat and say, “Bout damn time. Ya’ll niggas out here sightseeing and shit. I am trying to be home before midnight.”

Moments later, Keith yells, “Adonis?”

“What’s up?” He answers.

“Man, she got you too?”

“Who?”

“That bitch Alexis.”

I walk over, pat him on the back and say, “What up bruh?”

I feel the fear racing in Keith’s vein when he hears my voice.

I take two steps backwards and knocks him to the ground.

I point to Tyrone and Adonis as they throw Rachel’s body in a resting place and yells, “When you finish wit dat hoe throw this bitch ass nigga with her.”

They hurriedly mix the cement and pour it. I stand over Keith and say, “You were a bad ass but now you will be a buried one.

Twenty minutes later Adonis grabs his feet and Tyrone clutches his hands and drag him to the hole.

“Yo Shafiq, what’s next?” Tyrone asks.

“I got an idea.” Adonis interjects.

“Hurry up, I got shit to do.” Shafiq responds.

“Make that nigga scratch his way out.” Adonis suggests.

"I don't give a fuck what you do to him." I respond sparking a blunt.

They put him on the hardened cement feet first and throw the turf grass around him.

"Damn, that shit dried fast." Tyrone says as Keith hands hangs over the hole.

Minutes later, Adonis smacks him in the face to wake him and says, "I have a soft spot tonight. Find your way home nigga."

See, Hear and Speak no Evil....

Chapter 30
(Bianca)

Sitting on the edge of the bed with a towel wrapped around my body deciding on the outfit for tonight. The more I stare in the closet the emotional I am.

"I never stopped loving him." Saying to myself with tears flowing.

I slowly remove my dress from the hanger and cry hysterically when the phone scare me.

"Hello." I answer through sniffing.

"Baby, are you okay?" Anthony asks.

"Yes, I am. Are you on the way?"

"Be there in fifteen minutes. I have a wonderful evening planned. I love you."

"I love you too."

I hurriedly disconnect the call, lotion/spray *Adrienne Vittadini* and prepare myself. I stand in the mirror with a *BeBe Black Asymmetrical Mock Dress, Black and Gold Addison Platform Sandals and Gold accessories.*

Putting the last touch of lipstick and the doorbell rings. I feel butterflies in my stomach as my feet tries to move. Finally, my hand and doorknob meet and open with a smile.

"Damn baby, you look breathtaking." Anthony immediately answers.

"Thank you, that is very sweet." I response blushing.

He comes in, interlocks his fingers with mine and closes the door.

"I miss you Bianca." He mentions kissing my neck.

Slowly releasing his hand and squirming a little bit, I responds, "I made reservations at *Emeril's Restaurant*. I hope that is okay."

"Anything for you." He answers with confusion.

"I miss you too." I finally admit calming him.

"Are you ready?"

"Yes, I am." I respond with a glow in my eyes.

We walk out the door and a driver stands outside of a limousine waiting.

"You didn't have to do all of this."

"I know I didn't have to but you deserve this and so much more."

Thinking to myself being escorted in the car, "Yeah he is definitely getting some pussy tonight."

§§§§§§§§§§§§§§§§§§§§§§§§§§§§§§§§

(Anthony)

I drape a tie around my neck and disclose, "Alright nigga time to use all of those college drama classes."

Several times during the past weeks, I was tempted to strangle her while she slept or sucking my dick. If only she knew how much I hate her.

I have waited years to destroy her mind and heart as much as she did mine. Tonight, is the start of performances of a lifetime and I will enjoy every scene.

I walk out of the door and my chariot awaits. I rented a *Black Cadillac Limousine* with a dozen of yellow roses symbolizing our new beginning.

I hand the chauffeur an envelope with his payment and instruction so we can begin our journey.

I place a call to Bianca to see if she is ready.

"Hello." She answers sniffing.

"Baby, are you okay?" I ask. But my mind says, "Bitch why the fuck are you crying?"

"Yes, I am. Are you on the way?"

"Be there in fifteen minutes. I have a wonderful evening planned. I love you."

"I love you too."

As soon as I end the call I know I am pulling her heartstrings.

We arrive to her house within twelve minutes and I exit to knock on the door.

She opens and I stand in disbelief for a few seconds.

"Damn baby, you are breathtaking." I blurt. "Now this is the woman that stole my soul in college."

"Thank you, Anthony, that is very sweet." She responds trying not to blush.

"I miss you Bianca." I say with soft kisses on her neck.

She slowly releases her hand and frowns as if my kisses disgust her but responds, "I made reservations at *Emeril's Restaurant*. I hope that is okay."

"Anything for you." I answer through clenched teeth. Thinking to myself, "How the hell you want to go to *Emeril* but act like you don't want to be touched. I should call this shit off and kill her ass right here.

"No no no," I whisper to myself shaking my head with closed eyes.

"I miss you too." She finally conveys.

"Are you ready?" I ask trying to ensure she thinks she did something with that fucked up response.

"Yes, I am."

She steps closer to me and says, "Baby, let me straighten your tie," and kisses my cheek.

I reach into my pocket and drop an envelope on the floor as we walk out the door. The driver stands outside of with a few roses in hand.

"You didn't have to do all of this." She says getting in the limo.

"I know I didn't have to but you deserve this and so much more." I respond quickly wiping the lipstick from my face.

She slides her hand on my lap and places her head on my shoulder.

I pour a glass of wine and say, "Let's make a little toast."

She takes the glass and announces, "Here's to the present and future."

We exchange words through the remainder of the ride until the car stops.

The driver opens the door and says, "Call me when you are ready."

I hold her hand to assist with exiting the limo and walk in the restaurant.

We are greeted by the staff and escorted to our table with a view overlooking the river.

As soon as I see the menus, my stomach drops at the prices but my compensation will be awarded in time.

"Do you see anything you like?" I ask.

"Baby these prices are high as hell."

"No price is too high for you Bianca."

She continues looking and I say, "I will be right back."

"I should be ready to order then."

I find the waiter, slip $100 bill and a package, "You know what to do."

He nods and turns into the kitchen.

I walk in the bathroom, splash water on my face and say with encouraging words, "You can do this!"

I slap my face twice and walk back to the table.

"Baby, you can order for us. I don't know what to get." She announces with a baffled look.

I signal for the waiter and says, "I am ready."

He responds with glasses of *Chardonnay*, "What else may I get you?"

"I would like the *Smoked Eggplant Bruschetta* for an appetizer, two entrees of *Sweet Barbecue Roasted Salmon* and a *Soft Pretzel Bread Pudding*."

As soon as the waiter leaves, I move my chair closer to Bianca and say, "Thank you."

"No need to thank me Anthony. I am happy to spend this evening with you."

We engage in small talk until our meal arrive covering the table.

Through the lip smacking, I pull an envelope out of my jacket and asks, "Are you serious about our future?"

She licks her fingers and answer, "Of course."

I slide it to her and say, "Our plane leaves in the morning."

"Plane? Morning?"

"I will be on that plane with or without you."

"This is not to California or something. You are talking about Morocco. With me?" She yells looking at the tickets.

"Yes, I am. Do you like your dessert?"

"Baby I am stuffed."

"Taste a little bit for me."

She sticks her fork in the bread pudding but it doesn't go through. She picks it up, look inside and move the creation around her surprise.

Tears flow as she finally sees and opens the box displaying a white and mocha engagement ring.

"Oh Anthony, I am speechless."

"Will you be my wife?"

"Of course I will." She answers jumping in my arms.

We continue our meals and drive to enjoy the rest of our evening.

"No need to go back to your place, we will get everything you need on the trip."

"Yes baby." She answers with kisses.

§§§§§§§§§§§§§§§§§§§§§§§§§§§§§§§§§§

(Alexis)

Sitting up in the bed and sees it is 2:30 am. I am getting worried. I know I can be abrasive sometimes but I don't want us to go another day without talking.

Pick up the phone again and it is still going straight to voicemail.

Look over seeing Shafiq sleep and I don't want to disturb him especially from his mission yesterday.

Slowly get out the bed, throw on some sweats and speed over to Bianca's house.

I look at the dash and now it is 3:30 am. She can't sleep that damn hard not to hear the phone ringing and her schedule is clear.

"You must be seriously pissed at me from our last conversation."

I speed to her house and let myself in with the spare key.

Nothing is out of place and I smell her soft scent in the rooms. I truly hope everything is okay.

I glance at her figurine on the table and notice an envelope on the floor addressed to me.

"What the fuck is this?" I say opening it.

"As careful as you try to be, I am more cunning than you. Now you will see how it feels to lose someone you love. If you can find us, then you can have her but it will be in pieces. Your move slut."

I stand in disbelief, shaking and fall to the floor crying.

"How much is the cost of Revenge"

3191

THANK YOU'S

To the *Universal Being* which governs my mind, body and spirit. This gift wouldn't have evolved without your water and sunlight. To my *Creolistic Ink* Family for pushing when I pulled and motivated when I wanted to give up. My ink pours from your love. To Photographer *Montrell Worsley* (IG: the_montrel_effect) with models *Korey Gandy* (IG: korey_gandy) and *CoCo Surratt* (IG: _feisty_); Photographer *Linwood Williams* of *Lenzcapture Photography* and model *Javanica Scott*; words can't describe the admiration I have for your originality and patience. To *Flenardo Taylor* for pounding on his chest to be heard through my irritation. To *Trika Green, Chandra Davis*, *Monique Riley*, *Joann Hawk*, *Letizia Payne*, *Antoinette Simmons*, *Lilly Miley-Catron* and *Dwayne Anthony* for many years of encouragement and conversations. To ALL my Supporters / Wett Wipers from Dubai to Rhode Island and all the lovely states in between. I am speechless from your never-ending love and smiles while being my undercover muse. SPECIAL THANKS to Chane` Sykes for bringing order, grown-folk jokes and peeks of nudity to break the monotony. (I swear I can't make my life up LOL)

Once again, THANK YOU, for enjoying another phase of my creativity. Or is it?

www.ingramcontent.com/pod-product-compliance
Lightning Source LLC
Chambersburg PA
CBHW060219180626
46813CB00007B/2891
9780692873137